FROM THE
NANCY DREW FILES

THE CASE: *Find the maniac driver who mowed down Kim Baylor in broad daylight. Is he connected with the mysterious Rosita that Nancy heard Kim talking about?*

SUSPECTS: *Ricardo, a lifeguard with a mean streak. He knows Kim, but he's not looking to be helpful.*

Rosita—Nancy's found her photo in Kim's hotel room, but the girl seems to have disappeared.

Dirk Bowman is blond and blue eyed, with a perfect tan and a perfect body. He's very interested in Nancy and the case—maybe too interested.

COMPLICATIONS: *Kim is near death, and the top suspect has just been murdered. Nancy, George, and Bess set out to trap the killer on a midnight sail—a cruise that turns out to be a party to nowhere.*

Books in The Nancy Drew Files® Series

Available from ARCHWAY Paperbacks

THE
NANCY DREW
FILES™ (CASE • 5

HIT AND RUN
HOLIDAY

Carolyn Keene

AN ARCHWAY PAPERBACK
Published by POCKET BOOKS

New York London Toronto Sydney Tokyo Singapore

AN ARCHWAY PAPERBACK *Original*

An Archway Paperback published by
POCKET BOOKS, a division of Simon & Schuster Inc.
1230 Avenue of the Americas, New York, NY 10020

ISBN: 0-671-73660-4

First Archway Paperback printing November 1986

16 15 14 13 12 11 10

NANCY DREW, AN ARCHWAY PAPERBACK and colophon
are registered trademarks of Simon & Schuster Inc.

THE NANCY DREW FILES is a trademark
of Simon & Schuster Inc.

Printed in the U.S.A.

IL 6+

HIT AND RUN HOLIDAY

Chapter

One

$\mathbf{W}$E MADE IT!" Nancy Drew said with a grin. "Fort Lauderdale, here we are!"

Gripping the wheel in eager anticipation, Nancy turned the rental car onto Route A1A, a coastal highway lined with tall, swaying palm trees. To the left was a seemingly endless string of hotels and motels, fast-food places, restaurants, and discos. To the right, shimmering in the late morning sun, was a broad beach of nearly white sand, and beyond that, the sparkling blue-green waters of the Atlantic Ocean.

Beside Nancy, George Fayne gazed out the window at the beach. "I can't wait to get into that water," she said. "I may never come out except to eat."

"Who cares about the water?" Bess Marvin, George's cousin, said with a giggle. "Just look at all those tan male bodies out there! I've already counted nine that I could fall in love with." As their car passed a group of boys crossing the street, Bess turned around and looked out the back window. "Make that twelve," she said excitedly.

Nancy glanced into the rearview mirror and laughed. "Help me find our hotel first," she suggested. *"Then* you can check out the boys."

Early that morning, the three friends had left the cold March sleets of River Heights and flown to the south of Florida, joining thousands of other young people on spring break who poured into Fort Lauderdale in search of sun, sand, fun, and romance.

Actually, Bess was the only one who was looking to fall in love. George was still attached to Jon Berntsen, a boy she'd met on a ski trip, and Nancy's relationship with Ned Nickerson was in good shape at the moment. Nancy knew that Bess, with her blond hair and pretty figure, would probably have a date in fifteen minutes flat; while slender, athletic, dark-haired George was sure to set some kind of swimming, volleyball, or surfing record. As for herself, Nancy was looking just to have fun and go home with a great tan.

In her last case, *Smile and Say Murder,* she'd discovered that the world of publishing could be deadly, when she'd exposed a clever plot that included murder. So a Florida vacation seemed the perfect way to unwind.

"There it is," she said, pointing to a gleaming white stucco building. "The Surfside Inn. They were right—every room has a window facing the ocean."

"And the boys," Bess said with a sigh.

"Let's hurry and change so we can hit the beach," Nancy suggested, as she pulled the car into a tight parking space on a side street next to the hotel.

"What do you mean, 'we'?" George asked with a laugh. "You've got a case to solve, remember?"

Nancy laughed, too. "It's not a case," claimed the young detective. "I'm just checking up on Kim. It'll take me all of five minutes."

Kim Baylor, a friend of all three girls, had been in Fort Lauderdale for ten days. Just before Nancy left River Heights, Kim's mother had called and told her that Kim had decided to stay on an extra week. Mrs. Baylor wasn't really worried, she said, she simply wanted Nancy to drop by Kim's hotel and see that everything was all right. She'd felt that Kim had sounded odd over the phone, but thought she was probably just being an over-protective parent.

"I bet I can solve your mystery for you without even talking to Kim," Bess told Nancy as they piled out of the car. "It's simple—Kim met a fabulous guy and she's staying on because she's madly in love." Bess tugged two canvas bags from the back of the car, then stared across the street at a tall, well-muscled boy running toward the ocean. "Just look at him," she said dreamily. "What couldn't *I* do with an extra week down here!"

"Stop drooling and help us carry the bags inside," George joked. "The sooner we get changed, the sooner you can start looking for Mr. Right."

The hotel room wasn't large or luxurious, but it had everything the girls needed, and besides, none of them planned to spend much time in it. In ten minutes, they had changed out of their travel clothes and into their swimsuits. Bess had brought six, and for her first trip to the sun and sand, she put on a blazing pink bikini that showed off her figure perfectly.

George, who was wearing a blue-and-white-striped tank suit cut very high on the legs, gave Bess a wry smile. "Nobody's going to have any trouble seeing you," she commented. "Not in that color."

"That's the whole point," Bess replied seriously. Then she sighed as she looked at Nancy, whose blue-green bikini was the perfect color for her reddish blond hair and made her slim legs look miles long. "I just wish I had your figure," Bess told her enviously.

"You don't have to worry," Nancy assured her. "I'm not down here for the guys, remember? And even if I were, you have half an hour before I even show up on the beach."

Bess grabbed a large beach towel. "What do you mean?"

"I've decided to drop by Kim's hotel first," Nancy explained. She found her beach bag and tossed in everything she could possibly need on the beach: sunglasses, suntan lotion, a book, her Walkman, and even an extra bikini. Then she threw on a short cover-up made of soft white cotton. She started toward the door. "I thought I'd solve my 'case' first," she said with a grin. "But after that—look out, Lauderdale!"

Kim's hotel, the Vistamar, turned out to be just three blocks away from the Surfside, and it should have taken Nancy about two minutes to reach it. Instead, it took closer to ten. The sidewalks were jammed with kids heading for the beach or just strolling along, stopping to strike up a conversation with anyone who caught their eye.

Girls were checking out boys, boys were checking out girls, and Nancy lost count of how many surfing, swimming, and disco dates she turned down. She saw plenty of great-looking guys she wouldn't have minded spending time with, but because of Ned, she wasn't really tempted. Still, it was fun just being in the middle of it all, and as she spotted Kim's hotel, she thought that Bess was probably right—Kim must have met somebody special, and she wanted to be with him for as long as possible.

The Vistamar was on a narrow side street just off the main road. It was lime green, five stories high, and when Nancy went in, she just missed the elevator. However, since Kim's room was on the second floor, she climbed the stairs. She found room 207 easily and was just about to knock when she heard Kim's voice through the partially open door.

"Don't blame me, Ricardo!" Kim cried urgently. "I don't know how they found out, but they did!"

There was a pause, and when she didn't hear Ricardo answer, Nancy figured Kim must be talking on the phone. She tried not to eavesdrop, but Kim sounded so frantic it was hard not to hear her.

"I told her not to leave!" Kim went on. "She knew she wasn't supposed to, but . . . I don't know, Ricardo, maybe she got cabin fever or something. What difference does it make? She's gone!"

Nancy wasn't even trying not to listen anymore. Who was gone? she wondered. Kim hadn't come down with a girlfriend. Nancy knew that. But even if she'd taken on a roommate, what was the business about not leaving the room?

Kim lowered her voice, and Nancy leaned closer to the door. That was when she noticed it—not only was the door ajar, but the lock had obviously been broken. It hadn't been a very smooth job, either. The metal looked as if it had been gouged with a screwdriver, and the wood around it was splintered. Whoever had broken it must have wanted to get inside in a hurry.

Nancy didn't have a clue as to what was going on, and she waited impatiently for Kim to finish talking so she could find out.

"Don't say that, you're scaring me," Kim protested. She waited, then sighed. "All right, okay. I'll meet you at your perch in ten minutes."

Perch? Nancy almost smiled. Was Ricardo a boy or a bird? When she heard Kim say goodbye, she started to knock again. But the door was flung open before she had a chance, and a very startled Kim Baylor was staring at her.

"Nancy!" Kim's brown eyes widened in surprise. "What are you doing here?"

7

"I told you I might come down, remember?" Nancy said. "Besides, your—"

"Oh, that's right," Kim interrupted. "So much has been going on, I guess I forgot." She was already out the door and hurrying down the hall toward the elevator. "Listen, I can't talk now, I'm in a rush. But I really do want to see you. Maybe when I—"

"Hey, where's the fire?" Nancy joked as Kim kept jabbing at the elevator button. "Let's take the stairs, and then I'll walk you wherever you're going. We can talk on the way." She hurried to keep up with her friend, who was already at the stairs. "Kim, what's going on? You look freaked, to say the least."

Kim hurried down the stairs, her rubber beach sandals slapping on the cement. "I *am* freaked," she called over her shoulder. "You just won't believe what's been happening!"

"Try me," Nancy suggested.

"I will, I will, but, Nancy, it's just too complicated to get into right now. I've got something really important to do, but I promise I'll tell you everything as soon as I can."

Frustrated, Nancy followed Kim through the hotel's small, deserted lobby toward the street door. Kim dashed outside. Nancy ran after her, but her sandal chose that moment to slip off her foot. She bent over, put it back on, and hurried after her friend.

Kim was standing impatiently on the curb,

her long brown hair blowing in the sea breeze. She reached up, pulled a strand of hair out of her eyes, and stepped into the street.

Nancy was just leaving the hotel when she heard the sound of a car's engine firing and the squeal of tires as the car peeled away. She saw that Kim had reached the middle of the street. Nancy started after her, but it was at that second that she noticed the dark blue car racing toward Kim.

Nancy yelled but it was too late. The car was barreling down the street at a crazy speed. Kim opened her mouth to scream, but her voice was drowned out by the sound of the impact.

The car never slowed down. Its tires squealed again as it sped around the corner and out of sight.

Chapter

Two

IN A SECOND, Nancy was at Kim's side. It was impossible to tell how badly her friend was hurt. All Nancy could see were cuts and scrapes, but she didn't dare move her. She wasn't even going to take the chance of putting her friend's head in her lap. She knelt down, took Kim's hand, and leaned close to her.

"Kim?" Nancy tried to keep her voice from shaking. "It's going to be okay. Just don't move."

Gripping Nancy's hand, Kim licked her lips and tried to say something. Her voice was so weak that Nancy could barely hear her.

"Rosita," Kim whispered. "The . . . it was . . . Rosita." She took another breath and started to say something more, but then her eyelids fluttered closed and she was silent.

Nancy looked up and was surprised to see that a crowd of ten or fifteen people had gathered. She'd been concentrating so hard on Kim that she hadn't even noticed them.

"Could someone call an ambulance, please?" Nancy asked.

An elderly man nodded his head. "Of course," he said, and hurried away.

A voice close to Nancy asked, "Is she dead?"

The person who'd asked about Kim was a young woman, wearing the uniform of a hotel maid.

Nancy swallowed hard and shook her head. "No, she's not dead," she told her. "She's breathing. But she passed out."

The woman nodded and started to leave.

"Wait!" Nancy called. "Did you see what happened?"

"No, I didn't," the woman said. "I was inside. I heard a scream, but that's all. I came out to see, and on the way, I told my boss to call the police. It sounded like a bad accident."

"It was bad," Nancy agreed grimly. "But it wasn't an accident."

"I wouldn't know about that, miss," the woman said, backing away. "I have to go to work now."

In the distance, Nancy could hear the wail of

a siren, and she knew help was on the way. Still holding Kim's hand, she glanced up at the other people. "Did anyone see it happen?" she asked. "Did anyone see who was driving the car?"

A few people shook their heads, but no one said anything.

I couldn't have been the only one on the sidewalk, Nancy thought in frustration. Somebody must have seen something.

She knew they couldn't have gotten the license plate number, though. In those few awful seconds before the car hit Kim, Nancy had noticed that it didn't have a front plate, and as it tore off down the street, she realized that the back plate was missing too. But she'd been in such a hurry to get to Kim that she hadn't taken the time to look for anything else.

"How about the make of car or the year?" Nancy asked the onlookers. "Or whether it had two doors or four doors?"

A few more heads were shaken.

"Anything?" Nancy asked desperately. "This is important. Didn't anyone see *anything?*"

Nancy scanned the crowd, trying to catch a sympathetic eye. At the edge of the group she noticed a young guy, about nineteen or twenty, wearing a black swimsuit. He was one of the handsomest boys Nancy had ever seen, with black hair and eyes and smooth, dark gold skin. But it wasn't his looks that caught her attention—it was the expression in his eyes. He'd been staring at Kim, but as Nancy watched he raised his head and glanced down the street, in the direction the car had gone. His eyes glittered, and his lips curled into a tight smile.

What kind of smile? Nancy wondered. An angry smile? A satisfied one?

But Nancy didn't have time to do more than wonder. Its siren shrill and piercing, a police car rounded the corner, followed by an ambulance. The moment they came into sight, the crowd scattered, leaving Nancy alone with Kim.

"It was a hit and run," she told the officer who hurried over to her. "The car didn't bother to slow down for a second."

The policeman nodded and began firing questions at Nancy. What was Kim's name, where was she staying, where was she from? Nancy answered and then told him all she could about the accident, which wasn't much. "There were a lot of people around," she finished, "but they all split the minute they saw your car."

Closing his pad, the policeman nodded again. "Illegals, probably," he said. "Afraid to get involved."

Nancy suddenly understood. If people were in the country illegally, they'd rather keep their mouths shut than come forward and tell what they saw. Because if they had to testify in court, they'd be discovered, and then it would be goodbye, U.S.A.

Nancy looked over at Kim, who was being lifted gently onto a stretcher. "I can't believe this is happening," she said, feeling both sorry for the illegals and frustrated with them. "My friend gets run down in front of half a dozen witnesses, but I'm the only one who sees anything."

"Yeah, it's tough," the officer agreed. "There's a lot of ugly business going on down here in paradise."

Kim was being loaded into the ambulance by then. One of the medics jumped in after her.

"What about the car?" Nancy asked. "Do you think you'll find it?"

"There's not much to go on," the officer replied frankly. "But we'll give it our best shot."

"Okay," said Nancy. She climbed into the back of the ambulance and settled herself next to Kim. The medic closed the doors, and the ambulance pulled away, its siren going full blast.

Nancy thought about what the officer had meant—that if the car ever did turn up, it would probably be weeks later, in a junkyard somewhere. If they were lucky.

But Nancy wasn't going to put her trust in luck. She might return to River Heights with her skin as winter-pale as when she left, but she was going to find out why her friend was deliberately run over on a bright, sunny day in the middle of paradise.

It was two o'clock by the time Nancy left the hospital. Kim was still unconscious, but the doctors were almost certain she'd be okay— the worst they could find were a bad concussion and a broken wrist. Nancy had called Kim's mother, and Mrs. Baylor had said she'd be down later that afternoon if she had to hijack a plane to get there.

As Nancy walked down the street, she suddenly realized she was famished. She bought a hot dog from a stand on a street corner and wolfed it down while she headed toward Kim's hotel. What she really wanted to do was jump in the ocean and swim until her nerves stopped jangling. But she couldn't relax, not then. There was too much to find out. What kind of dangerous business had Kim gotten mixed up in? Why had the lock on her door been broken? Who was Ricardo? Who was Rosita?

Nancy knew that Kim's room just might hold some of the answers to those questions, so she tried to ignore the gorgeous beach only yards away from her. She also tried to ignore

15

the gorgeous boys around her, but it wasn't easy.

"Hey," one of them said, "you look frazzled. I just happen to know a nice, secluded little spot half a mile down the beach . . ."

"Hey, you're going to look like a cooked lobster soon if you're not careful," another one told her. "I'll be glad to rub in your suntan lotion personally!"

Nancy turned them down, but even though she was worried about Kim, she couldn't help smiling. Bess must be in absolute heaven, she thought. She glanced over at the crowded beach and realized that Bess and George didn't even know about Kim yet. I'll tell them later, she thought. First I've got to get a look at that hotel room. Remembering the broken lock, she figured it wouldn't be too hard.

Nancy bounded up the stairs again instead of waiting for the elevator. Quietly she pushed open the door and stepped into the hall. Good. It was empty.

Nancy kept her fingers crossed that it would stay that way. The last thing she wanted was to be seen nosing around Kim's room. She didn't have any idea yet whom she was up against, and until she found out, she couldn't trust a soul.

When Nancy reached room 207, she checked to make sure she was still alone, then put her hand on the doorknob, expecting it to turn easily.

The knob didn't turn at all. The door was locked.

Great, Nancy thought, just what I don't need—an efficient hotel. She didn't have her credit cards with her, so she couldn't force the lock that way. She rummaged through her beach bag, trying to find something thin and made out of metal.

No luck. The only hardware she had was the small hook in the top of her extra bikini.

Well, why not? she thought. It took five minutes, but finally Nancy had the metal hook free of the cloth. She spent another minute unbending it, and at last she held a thin metal probe about as long as her little finger. If this works, she told herself, you will have set some sort of record for ingenuity.

Grinning, Nancy gently slid the "pick" into the keyhole.

Suddenly the knob turned, and the door started to open. Nancy was about to congratulate herself when she realized that she didn't have anything to do with it. Someone—who probably didn't belong there—was inside Kim's room. And Nancy and the intruder were about to come face-to-face.

Chapter

Three

QUICKLY NANCY DROPPED her pick into her beach bag, stepped away from the door, and put on a confused expression, as if she were having trouble finding her room.

The door opened a little more, and a young man stuck his head out. In his left hand he held a very long pointed screwdriver. When he saw Nancy, his jaw hardened and his blue eyes turned icy. Nancy considered asking him what he was doing in the room, but his look stopped her. He might be involved in Kim's "accident," and if he was, Nancy didn't want him suspicious of her.

"Oh, hi!" she said casually. "Can you tell me where room three-twelve is?"

Opening the door just wide enough to let himself out, the guy gave Nancy a long, cold look, then finally raised his chin and glanced at the ceiling.

Nancy looked up too, pretending she didn't understand what he was trying to tell her. She noticed that he was wearing dark green pants and a matching shirt, the kind of uniform maintenance people wear. He must work for the hotel, Nancy thought, which was why he'd been in Kim's room. He'd probably just fixed the lock.

"Oh!" she said, as if the light had finally dawned on her. "I'm on the wrong floor, huh?"

Nodding briefly, the guy pulled the door shut behind him, and then stood there, obviously waiting for her to leave.

Nancy heard the lock click and was glad she'd been prepared. Smiling brightly, she said, "No wonder I couldn't find three-twelve! Thanks!"

"Mr. Friendly" glared at her again and finally headed for the stairs, so Nancy stood in front of the elevator, pretending to push the button. When she heard the last echo of his footsteps, she rushed back to room 207, fished out her pick, and went to work.

In just a couple of minutes, Nancy was inside Kim's room.

It was a total disaster. Clothes were everywhere—hanging out of drawers, strewn across the floor, even spilling from the wastepaper basket. Postcards, paperbacks, makeup, and skin lotion were ripped, scattered, or overturned. The sheets were on the floor, and the mattress was half off the bed.

It was not the mess made by someone who was having too good a vacation to bother picking things up. It wasn't even the mess made by a slob, Nancy thought. It was the kind of mess made by somebody who was looking for something.

Nancy didn't have to wonder who had searched the room. It must have been handsome "Mr. Friendly," the stone-faced maintenance man. No wonder he'd given her such a dirty look when he found her lurking outside the room. Obviously he didn't work for the hotel, but just who did he work for? Ricardo? Rosita?

For a moment, Nancy was tempted to go after him, but then she decided it would be a waste of time. People who trashed hotel rooms didn't wait around to answer questions. Mr. Friendly was long gone. She hoped.

The thing to do was figure out what he'd been looking for.

Afraid that somebody might be watching the hotel room, Nancy left the shades down and the lights off. The fluorescent bulb in the bathroom was enough to see by. Not even sure where to begin, she started wading through the piles of clothes and paperbacks on the floor. A piece of newspaper caught in her sandal; as she picked it up she noticed the headline of a story about illegal aliens.

The story had been circled in red ink, and Nancy figured Kim had done it. Kim was like that—always interested in the underdog. If I keep my eyes peeled, Nancy thought with a smile, I'll probably find a letter she wrote to the editor, saying what a rotten situation the illegals are in.

But Nancy wasn't getting anywhere. She tossed the paper toward the wastebasket and headed for the bathroom. Medicine cabinets were such obvious hiding places, maybe Mr. Friendly hadn't bothered to look there.

No luck. The "maintenance" man had pulled out every jar, bottle, and tube, and left them piled in the sink. Even the toothbrushes were out of their holders, lying like two pickup sticks on the fake marble vanity top.

Nancy was halfway out the bathroom when it hit her—*two* toothbrushes. She walked back in and took another look. Right, two of them —one blue and obviously well used; the other red, without a single bent bristle.

Kim didn't have a roommate, she reminded herself. Or did she? Nancy looked more carefully at the countertop. One bottle each of shampoo and conditioner. One tube of toothpaste, one can of deodorant. Two hairbrushes, one full of light brown strands, the other with several strands of long black hair caught in it.

Okay, Nancy thought. Kim might have bought a second toothbrush, but there was no way she could have used that other hairbrush. And if she hadn't come to Florida with a roommate, then she'd invited some girl to stay with her once she got there.

Nancy walked back into the main room, looking for more evidence of that roommate, and she found it in the wastepaper basket. A skirt and blouse—cotton, homemade, no labels, muddy, and wrinkled. They must have been pretty once, but Nancy knew they didn't belong to Kim. For one thing, they weren't her style. Kim would never have worn them. For another, Kim hated sewing; she'd wait until every last button had fallen off a blouse before picking up a needle and thread.

Nancy was frowning at the skirt and blouse when she heard footsteps in the hall. When they stopped outside the door, she sank down behind the bed as quietly as possible, listening. Was it the maintenance man? Had he gotten suspicious of her and come back? The footsteps shuffled around, then faded away.

As Nancy let her breath out, her head dropped, and she found herself staring at a strip of photo-booth snapshots lying on the rug at her feet. Picking it up gingerly, as if it might suddenly disintegrate, Nancy studied the strip of photos. The first was of Kim alone, mugging for the camera; the second was of Kim and another girl. All the rest were of the second girl, who was very pretty, with long black hair, but who never smiled and who looked into the camera with frightened, suspicious dark eyes. "Rosita," Nancy whispered to herself. "She has to be Rosita."

Nancy examined the photograph intently, as if by staring hard enough she could bring Rosita to life and ask her all the questions that were spinning through her mind. How did you meet Kim? Why did Kim share her room with you? Who's Ricardo? Who was that phony maintenance man? Just exactly what did Kim mean when she lay in the street and whispered, "It was Rosita"?

Frustrated, Nancy stood up and began pacing the hotel room, still holding the strip of photos. Where was she going to find the answers to those questions? Who was she going to ask? Kim was still unconscious, and the only other person she thought might be involved was Mr. Friendly. She could hardly ask him, if she ever saw him again.

Well, at least she had something to go on, she thought, looking at the photograph. If she had to, she'd wander up and down the beach, asking anybody and everybody if they'd seen that girl. I'll find you, Rosita, Nancy thought. And when I do, you'd better have some good answers.

Dropping the strip of photos into her beach bag, Nancy took one last look around the torn-up room and then headed for the door. Her hand was on the knob when she heard footsteps in the hall again.

Nancy dropped her hand, figuring she'd rather not be seen, no matter who was out there. The footsteps came closer and then stopped right outside room 207. Nancy stepped backward, her eyes on the door. It could be somebody who really does work for the hotel, she told herself. A maid, maybe, coming to clean up the room. The doorknob jiggled. Then Nancy heard the sound of a key sliding slowly into the lock. No maid would unlock a door like that, Nancy thought. Besides, a maid would knock first. Whoever was unlocking that door was probably looking up and down the hall, making sure no one was watching. Whoever was out there didn't want to be seen.

The doorknob turned. In three quick strides, Nancy was across the room and in the closet, hiding behind the few clothes that were left hanging there. Just as the outer door swung open, Nancy pulled the closet door closed, leaving a half-inch crack to see through.

Because the room was so dim, all Nancy could glimpse at first was a tall, shadowy figure silhouetted against the pale wall. It stood there for a few seconds, obviously sizing up the situation. Then, slowly, it moved away from the door and into the center of the room. Nancy held her breath as it passed the closet and walked cautiously toward the bathroom.

Whoever it was didn't turn on any lights, and Nancy knew she'd been right—the person didn't work for the hotel, even though he or she had a key, and definitely didn't want to be discovered.

For an instant, the figure was framed in the bathroom light, and Nancy saw it from the back: It was the figure of a dark-haired boy, wearing a black bathing suit and a T-shirt, and carrying what looked like a small canvas bag. Nancy opened the closet door a little wider, hoping to get a better look, but by then, the boy was out of the light. In that instant, though, Nancy decided that he looked uncomfortably familiar. Something about his build and the way he held his head reminded her of the handsome boy at the scene of the hit and run, the one who'd smiled so mysteriously and then disappeared.

Was the intruder really the same boy? Nancy wondered. Then she realized that it didn't matter, not at the moment. What mattered was that the boy, who had walked all around the room, and had been in and out of the bathroom, was headed for the closet in which Nancy was hiding. His hand was outstretched, reaching for the doorknob.

Chapter
Four

NANCY STAYED ABSOLUTELY still, not even daring to breathe. At the last second, the boy shook his head, apparently changing his mind about the closet, and returned to the bathroom.

Nancy exhaled a long, shaky, silent breath. She had gathered one more important piece of information. The intruder was definitely the same handsome boy she had seen after Kim's accident.

Nancy could hear him rummaging around in the bathroom, picking things up and putting them down again. Were he and the maintenance man working together? Had the maintenance man seen Nancy enter Kim's room and told the boy to follow her?

Silently Nancy eased back into the darkness of the closet. She couldn't let herself get caught, and she wished her heart would stop beating so hard.

The boy left the bathroom, dropping a few things into the canvas bag. They clattered against each other as they landed, and Nancy thought they must be jars. Makeup? Lotion? What would he want with Kim's makeup and hand lotion?

Again the intruder stepped toward the closet. Nancy took her hand off the knob, afraid she might shake the door, and held her breath again. What would he do if he found her? What would *she* do?

The boy stopped in front of the closet, and Nancy gripped the strap of her beach bag, figuring she could swing it at his face and make a run for it if she had to. Her hand was sweaty and a muscle in her leg started jumping. She wished he'd do whatever he was going to do so she could move. Anything was better than waiting.

Finally he did move. But not to the closet. Nancy heard a strange shuffling sound, and she peered through the opening.

The boy was bending over, grabbing a few pieces of scattered clothing and stuffing them into his bag. As Nancy watched, he straightened up, his back still to her, and then swiftly walked to the door, opened it, and stepped outside.

Nancy forced herself to count slowly to five. She wanted to give him enough time to reach the stairs or the elevator and think he was safe. Then she'd follow him and try to find out who he was and what he was doing in Kim's room.

At the count of five, she let herself out of the stuffy closet, crossed the room, and opened the door. The hall was empty. The elevator was stopped on the third floor. Nancy raced for the stairs and paused, listening. Two flights below, she heard a door open. Noises from the lobby drifted up to her before it closed again.

That's him, Nancy thought, rushing down the stairs. He won't be any farther than the street door by the time I get there. On the ground floor, she shoved open the door, nearly collided with a bellboy, and dashed across the lobby and out to the sidewalk.

The street looked almost the same as it had earlier that day, bright with sunlight and busy with vacationers heading for the ocean. Nancy glanced quickly in both directions, thought she saw the black-suited intruder turn onto the main avenue that ran along the beach, and swiftly made her way through the happy, sun-tanned crowds.

At the corner, Nancy stopped short, looking wildly in every direction. The main street was packed, the beach was packed. She counted at least fifteen guys in brief black bathing suits and was standing there wondering which one to go after first, when someone called her name.

"Nancy! Nancy, over here!"

Nancy looked across the street and saw Bess and George waving to her from the edge of the beach. Only a few hours had gone by since they'd all been together, changing into their swimsuits, but it seemed like days. She took another look at the crowded beach. Suddenly it seemed as if every boy was wearing a black bathing suit. Shaking her head, Nancy crossed the street and joined her friends.

"I thought you said you'd solve your 'case' in ten minutes," George teased. "What happened, couldn't you find Kim?"

"I found her," Nancy said. "Kim's—"

"Well, it's about time you got here!" Bess broke in. "We thought you'd decided to spend your entire vacation indoors. Nancy," she went on with a big smile, "meet Dirk Bowman. He owns a boat, and he's promised to take us all along on a midnight cruise. Doesn't that sound fantastic?"

Nancy turned and smiled distractedly at Dirk. She hadn't noticed him at first, but she should have guessed that Bess would have found someone by then.

"I don't actually own the boat, I just work for the lady who does," Dirk explained as he smiled back at Nancy. He was a fabulous-looking guy—sandy blond hair, deep blue eyes, and a perfect tan on a nearly perfect body. "But the invitation for the cruise is good. You have my word."

"It sounds great," Nancy told him. "But I don't think I'll be able—"

"Oh, come on, Nan," Bess protested. "We came down here to have fun, right? What could be more fun than a midnight cruise?"

"Really, it sounds great," Nancy said again, "but—"

"What is it, Nancy?" George asked. "You hardly look like somebody who's having a terrific time."

Nancy brushed her hair back and took a deep breath. "You're right. I'm not having a terrific time," she said. "But I'm afraid Kim's having a worse one." She glanced at the three of them and then went on to tell what had happened to their friend that morning.

"Oh, how awful!" Bess said in a horrified voice. "What kind of creep would run over somebody and keep on going?"

"I don't know," Nancy replied. "But I plan to find out. I don't think it was just some jerk who hit Kim and then panicked. I think it was deliberate. I think Kim got mixed up in something dangerous down here and she nearly paid for it with her life."

"What could she have gotten mixed up in?" George asked.

"I don't know yet," Nancy admitted. "But I plan to soon. Some very strange things have been going on." She told them about Kim's hotel room and the mess it was in, about the phony maintenance man, the snapshots of the pretty girl, and the guy who'd broken into the room and taken some clothes.

As she talked, Nancy noticed that Dirk Bowman was becoming extremely interested in what she was saying.

"Sounds like your vacation's not exactly turning out the way you expected," he commented when Nancy finished.

"Not exactly," Nancy agreed.

"Well, from what Bess and George have told me about you," he went on, "I'd bet you're not going to give up until you have all the answers." He smiled at Bess, and Nancy noticed that he had a dimple just to the left of his mouth. Bess looked enchanted. "Don't worry," Dirk went on, "they didn't talk about you that much. They just said that you're a detective, and you don't give up without a fight."

"I guess I don't," Nancy said. "And I sure won't give up on this case, not when one of my friends is lying in a hospital." She turned to Bess and George. "Kim's mother is flying down later today. I think we ought to be at the hospital when she gets there, don't you?"

"Absolutely," George said, and Bess nodded and sighed. "Poor Kim," she exclaimed. "I just can't believe it!"

"Listen," Dirk said to Nancy, "if there's anything I can do, I wish you'd let me know." He put a hand on Nancy's shoulder and flashed his dimple at her. "I know my way around Fort Lauderdale pretty well. Besides," he added, "I'm sort of a mystery nut. I'd really like to help you."

"Well, thanks." Nancy was aware that Dirk still had his hand on her shoulder, and she tried to shrug it off, but it stayed put.

"Listen," said Dirk, "that midnight cruise is probably out for you tonight, Nancy. I know you've got to be with your friend. But maybe you and I could get together tomorrow sometime and talk about this. I'd really like to help."

"I . . . I'm not sure," Nancy said, suddenly uncomfortable. "I don't know what I'll be doing tomorrow."

"I understand," Dirk replied with another charming, sympathetic smile. "But I'd really like to talk to you about all this."

"Well, I'll have to see." Nancy frowned.

Dirk seemed to have forgotten about Bess. It wasn't exactly cool, she thought, to dump somebody so fast.

Bess obviously didn't think it was too cool, either. Her eyes were flashing as she looked angrily at Dirk. Fortunately, George caught the look and decided that Bess better leave before she exploded. "Come on," she said, "let's get back to the hotel and change so we can go to the hospital."

"All right," Bess agreed.

"Hey, I'm free all morning tomorrow," Dirk said softly to Nancy. "Why don't I give you a call?"

Nancy felt more and more uncomfortable. She was just about to give Dirk a real brush-off, when he pulled her around to face him.

"I do know my way around Lauderdale," he said seriously, and Nancy noticed his sexy smile was gone. "If we can get together—privately—I think I might be able to give you a few tips about this mystery. You want to help your friend, don't you?"

"Of course I do!" Nancy said. "But right now, you're the one who's being mysterious. If you know something, why don't you just tell me?"

Dirk shook his head. "I would, believe me, but it's just not the right time or place. Besides, first I have to know everything you

34

know." Glancing past Nancy, Dirk seemed to see someone he recognized. He raised his arm in a greeting, then brought his hand down so that it was resting on the back of Nancy's neck. It was like a caress, Nancy thought, but there was nothing romantic about the look in his eyes. "Tomorrow, right?" he asked intently.

Nancy wasn't sure if Dirk was making a pass at her or if he really did know something about Kim. But she had to find out. "Okay," she finally agreed. "Tomorrow."

"Good." Dirk's smile returned, and giving Nancy's neck a gentle squeeze, he sauntered off to meet whomever it was he'd waved to.

Nancy watched him for a second, then turned to catch up with George and Bess. George was almost at the street, but Bess hadn't moved. She'd obviously been watching the whole thing, because she gave Nancy a confused look. Then she strode across the beach, completely ignoring the dozens of boys who tried to get her attention.

Nancy sighed and slipped off her sandals. She jogged across the warm sand toward Bess, trying to decide how to tell her that she didn't like—or trust—Dirk Bowman one bit.

Nancy was only a few yards from Bess when she suddenly stopped short, completely forgetting about Bess and Dirk for the moment. In front of her was a lifeguard's chair, and sitting in that chair was a handsome, bronze-skinned, dark-haired boy in a small black bathing suit. Nancy knew he was the guy she'd seen at the hit and run and rummaging around Kim's hotel room not half an hour earlier.

Nancy hoped nobody was drowning at the moment, because the guy sure wouldn't be any help—he couldn't take his eyes off her.

The only place he's seen you is at the hit-and-run scene, she reminded herself. He doesn't know you were in that hotel room, watching him.

Tossing her hair back, Nancy curved her lips in a slow smile and walked over to the lifeguard's chair.

"Hi, there," the lifeguard said when she reached him.

"Hello." Nancy noticed a small canvas beach bag at the foot of the chair. She would have given anything to see what was inside it. Still smiling, she said, "This is my first day in Lauderdale. Got any suggestions about how I should spend my time?"

The lifeguard raised his eyebrows. "Most people come here for the sun and the water," he said, in a slight Hispanic accent. "Isn't that what you came for?"

"Well, sure," Nancy told him. "Sun, surf, and . . . new friends, right?"

"Maybe." He gave her a teasing grin. "If you're lucky."

"Speaking of luck," Nancy went on, "one of my friends ran into a bad streak of it this morning. Or rather, it ran into her."

"Oh?"

"Yes. She was hit by a car, right in front of the Vistamar." Nancy kept her smile in place, trying not to sound too serious. "A lot of people were around. Maybe I'm wrong, but I thought I saw you there."

The lifeguard shifted in his chair, glanced out at the water, and then back at Nancy. His smile was gone, and his dark eyes were hard. "You're right," he said coldly. "You are wrong."

"Oh, well," Nancy said with a shrug. "My mistake."

The lifeguard didn't answer. He just stared at her a moment longer, then shifted his gaze back to the water.

He was lying, Nancy was sure. But there was no way she could prove it. Not yet. Figuring she'd only make him suspicious if she asked any more questions, she decided to drop the subject for the time being. She hitched her beach bag onto her shoulder and turned to leave.

Nancy was only about three feet away from the lifeguard's chair when she felt it—a sharp, burning pain in her left foot, as if she'd stepped on a red-hot needle. Gasping, she jerked her foot away and fell onto the sand. As she fell, she glanced up at the lifeguard. He was watching her, and his smile was back.

Chapter

Five

BITING HER LIP to keep from crying out, Nancy grabbed her foot and looked around to see what she'd stepped on. A few inches away she saw a large, bluish, slimy object partly covered by sand. It was a jellyfish, obviously, and as Nancy rubbed her foot, she wondered what kind it was and whether its poison was going to do any more damage than it already had.

A boy who'd seen her fall trotted over and prodded the jellyfish with a stick. "Portuguese man-of-war," he told her. "Ugly looking, huh?"

Nancy nodded. "What's going to happen

now?" she asked. "Is my foot going to shrivel up and fall off?" She was trying to joke, but the pain she felt was anything but funny.

The boy didn't look too amused either. "Well, I don't want to scare you," he said, "but I think you ought to hot-foot it to a doctor, excuse the pun."

Nancy suddenly remembered some stories about things like shock and unconsciousness. It's a good thing I'm on my way to the hospital, she thought. The boy offered her a hand, and she got to her feet, wincing. "Thanks."

"Any time," he told her. Glancing up at the lifeguard, he cupped his hands and called out, "Hey, Ricardo! You're falling down on the job, man. Why didn't you warn her these things are all over the beach today?"

Stunned, Nancy looked at the lifeguard too. So he was Ricardo. And his chair was the "perch" Kim had mentioned. No wonder he'd clammed up when she mentioned seeing him at the hit-and-run site. She wondered what he would have done if she'd told him about overhearing Kim's phone conversation with him, or seeing him sneaking around Kim's hotel room. Instead of letting me step on a jellyfish, he'd probably have tried to feed me to the sharks, she thought with a shudder.

At least she knew who the enemy was. All she had to do was find out why he was the enemy. Looking at Ricardo, who had made no apology and no move to help her, Nancy realized that deliberately letting her step on the man-of-war was his way of telling her to keep her nose out of his business.

You blew it, Ricardo, Nancy thought. Scaring me off doesn't work. And if you hadn't tried it, I might not have learned your name, and then I wouldn't come after you. But I will now.

Nancy started to walk away, stumbled, and nearly fell again. Her foot was beginning to go numb.

"Hey, you okay?" asked the boy who'd helped her up.

"No, but I'm sure I will be," Nancy told him. Then she raised her voice so that Ricardo could hear her. "I'll be fine. I'll be back, too. You can count on it."

As quickly as she could, Nancy made her way up the beach to her hotel. Bess and George had already changed, and when Nancy told them what had happened, they helped her change, then hustled her into the car and rushed her to the hospital emergency room as fast as possible. By the time they got there, the bottom of Nancy's foot was red and swollen, and the pain went clear up to her knee. But after checking her over, the doctor on duty said she'd be fine.

"You're lucky," she told her, as she rubbed some salve on Nancy's foot. "You must have

just one of its tentacles. If you'd
stung, your friends might have had
you in here."

ncy smiled in relief as the medicine
started to ease the stinging. The doctor gave
her the tube of salve, and after thanking her,
Nancy, Bess, and George took the elevator to
Kim's room. Kim's mother had just arrived,
and she greeted the three girls with tears in her
eyes.

"I just don't understand how this could have
happened!" Mrs. Baylor pulled a fresh tissue
from the box on Kim's bedside table and
wiped her eyes. "I was against this trip in the
first place. I should never have let her come!"

Nancy reached out to touch Mrs. Baylor's
arm. "You can't blame yourself," she said
gently.

"Oh, I know." Mrs. Baylor smoothed back
her hair and blew her nose. "I'm just so
worried. The police don't seem to be very
hopeful about finding the driver or the car.
They were nice, but I can tell they're not going
to spend a lot of time on this. Meanwhile, my
daughter's lying here unconscious!"

Nancy, Bess, and George stared at Kim, not
knowing what to say. The doctors had told
them that Kim was stable, that things looked
very promising for her. But she still hadn't
wakened, and it was hard to sit and just watch

her. It made them feel helpless, and *that* made them feel edgy.

Nancy was especially edgy. First of all, Kim's mother couldn't seem to stop crying. Not that Nancy blamed her. Her daughter had been run down; she had every right to cry. But all the sniffing and nose-blowing and sobbing made it hard to think. And Nancy needed to think. She was still in the dark about what was going on, despite the fact that she had two good leads—the picture of the girl and Ricardo. He was obviously mixed up in it, but how? And exactly what was he mixed up in? Maybe Dirk Bowman knew. His not-so-subtle hint made Nancy very curious, and she wished she could be with him at that very moment.

But one glance at Bess told Nancy that she'd better keep that wish to herself. Between the man-of-war sting and visiting Kim at the hospital, Nancy hadn't had a chance to explain things to her. Not that she had much explaining to do. She hadn't come on to the guy; he'd come on to her. Bess would realize that.

Actually, when Nancy thought about it, Dirk had started coming on to her as soon as she had mentioned what had happened to Kim. Perhaps he had more than just information for her. Nancy couldn't pass up a chance to learn something. She'd talk to Bess as soon as she could.

43

About the only thing not annoying Nancy was her foot. It was feeling better by the minute, so she knew she could make good on her promise to Ricardo—she'd be back. That was what was really making her edgy—she wanted to get out of the hospital and back on the trail.

"Oh, how lovely!" Mrs. Baylor exclaimed suddenly. Nancy glanced up and saw that a good-looking guy had just entered Kim's room carrying a big arrangement of flowers. He was wearing a brown uniform, so he must have been from a flower shop. He set the basket on the table, gave Kim a close look, then quickly left the room.

"That was so nice of you girls," Mrs. Baylor said tearfully.

George looked embarrassed. "Don't thank us," she said. "I'm afraid we didn't send them."

"Then who did?" mused Kim's mother.

Nancy reached over and carefully pushed aside the daisies and carnations, but she could find no card. Strange, she thought. Why would somebody send flowers without a card? And just who had sent them?

Kim's mother started to cry again. "This is like a nightmare," she sobbed. "Who on earth would want to hurt my daughter?"

"I don't know, Mrs. Baylor," Nancy told

her. "But I promise you, I'm going to find out."

When Dirk Bowman arrived at the Surfside Inn the next morning to pick her up, Nancy was sure of one thing—Bess was no longer upset with her. She understood what Nancy had to do. However, she was still hurt, and she was furious with Dirk for dumping her so rudely.

Nancy dressed casually in light cotton pants and a cotton shirt with a wild island print over her bikini. She wished she could wear her new sandals, but she put on her sneakers instead, since she wasn't sure what Dirk would end up showing her.

At precisely eleven o'clock, Dirk, lean and tan, showed up. Nancy greeted him, then stepped out with him into the fresh morning air.

"Ever been windsurfing?" Dirk asked, taking her hand and leading her toward a red sports car parked at the curb.

"No," Nancy told him. "I've surfed and I've sailed, but never at the same time." She liked his car, and she couldn't help admitting that she also liked the feel of his hand. Bess has great taste, she thought.

"Well, then, you'll probably catch on quickly," Dirk said with a dimpled smile. He put the car in gear and drove quickly down the street. "It's really terrific once you get the hang of it." For the next ten minutes, he kept up a steady, one-sided conversation about the joys of windsurfing.

It was all very interesting, Nancy thought, but it wasn't the information she was after. If Dirk really wanted to turn Nancy on, he'd tell her what he knew about Kim.

"Listen," she said, finally interrupting him. "I don't want to be rude, but you said you might be able to help me out on this case, that you might have some information for me."

"That's right," Dirk answered with an easy smile. "I might. But I told you, I need to know everything you know first."

Nancy was trying to decide what to tell him when Dirk parked the car, got out, and led her to a dock where an outboard boat loaded with two surfboards was tied. They jumped on, Dirk started the engine, and as they sped away, Nancy glanced back at the dock. Ricardo was standing there, watching them. Nancy felt a chill as she watched his figure grow smaller and smaller. What was Ricardo doing there, anyway? Had he followed her and Dirk? Were he and Dirk connected in some way?

It was impossible to talk over the buzz of the motor and the thumping of the waves as the boat plowed through the ocean, but Nancy did manage to ask Dirk where they were going.

When he answered her—telling her they were headed for a small island—he leaned so close she could smell his aftershave. He reminded her of Daryl Gray, a guy she'd almost fallen for. In fact, there was a lot about Dirk that reminded her of Daryl. He was gorgeous and friendly and would be easy to fall for too, but Nancy wasn't about to do that. She was after information, not involvement.

After twenty minutes, Dirk cut the motor and let the boat drift gently toward a sandy island dotted with palm trees. It shimmered in the sun, like a beautiful mirage.

"This is where we bring all the party-goers," he explained. "We drop them off around midnight and pick them up a few hours later. It's wild, sort of a big bash in the middle of nowhere."

Nancy nodded, remembering that he worked for some kind of excursion boat. As they beached the motorboat, she asked if he liked the job.

"It's great," he said. "And my boss, Lila Templeton, is one fun lady. Running these parties to nowhere isn't a job for her—she doesn't need one. Her boat is just a big toy. Ever eat a Templeton orange?"

"Probably," Nancy said.

"Well, every time you do, you're putting money in Lila's pocket. Her family owns half the citrus and sugarcane farms in Florida."

Nancy looked around. The island really is in the middle of nowhere, she thought. "Where does the party boat go after you drop everybody off?" she asked.

"Oh, it just cruises around." Dirk took Nancy's hand again and smiled at her. "I'm really glad you came out with me, you know. I wanted to be alone with you the minute I laid eyes on you, Detective."

Again Nancy noticed the warmth of his hand and the dimple alongside his mouth. Dirk Bowman was a real charmer, all right, but charm wasn't what she was after. "You called me 'detective,'" she pointed out, "so let's do some detecting, okay?"

With a laugh, Dirk agreed, so while they stripped down to their bathing suits, unloaded the surfboards, and unfurled the brightly colored sails, Nancy told him what had gone on the day before without giving away any important details. By the time she finished, they were on the boards, paddling away from the shore. "It's your turn," she said. "Tell me what *you* know."

Dirk sighed and shook his head. "Sorry, Detective. I'm afraid I came up with a great big zero."

Stunned, Nancy sat up, straddling the board. He never knew anything in the first place, she told herself furiously. It was just a line to get you out here, and you fell for it!

As if he read her mind, Dirk reached out and touched her knee. "Aw, come on, Detective. Don't be mad. I did ask around, but nobody knew anything. If I'd told you that this morning, you wouldn't have come with me, right?"

"Right," Nancy agreed instantly.

But Dirk didn't look insulted. Instead, he laughed. "Look at it this way. You're already in the water, so why not relax and let me teach you how to windsurf? It's the least I can do."

His laugh was hard for Nancy to resist, even with the thoughts of Ricardo and Kim and Rosita whirling through her mind. But she managed to keep a straight face. "One lesson, one ride," she said seriously. "That's it. Then we go back."

"You got it, Detective," Dirk promised. He went on to give her instructions about how to handle the board, how to pull up the sail, when to turn the boom, and how to bail out. "Always bail out backward, right onto your backside," he said. "That way the board won't break your skull."

Soon, Nancy was on her own, in deep water. Carefully she eased up from her stomach to her knees, reached into the water, and pulled up the sail. Keeping a tight grip on the boom, she got to her feet, found her balance, and stood up straight.

Wind filled the sail, and suddenly Nancy felt

49

as if she were flying over the water. She heard Dirk shouting encouragement and found herself laughing out loud as the board slapped over the waves. For just a moment, she forgot about everything but the sun and the wind and the salt spray.

Just when Nancy thought she was going as fast as it was possible to go, the board picked up speed. She wasn't sure if she could handle it, so she turned the boom, hoping to slow down. But she must have turned it the wrong way, because the sail was so full it looked ready to rip. Nancy decided to try one more time to slow down. If that didn't work, then she'd bail out.

Nancy turned the boom. Instantly, the pole fell over as if it had been snapped in two. The board tipped, pushing Nancy forward, and before she had time to react, she found herself hitting the water. Behind her, the heavy surfboard rose up like a sailfish leaping from the ocean. Then it started to fall—heading straight for Nancy's head.

Chapter

Six

NANCY TOSSED HER head back and desperately gulped in a mouthful of air. The board was falling fast; in a few seconds it would be on top of her. Nancy flipped sideways, kicked up with her legs, and felt the lethal board graze her thigh as she pulled herself deep under the water.

The current was strong; it somersaulted her over and over until she couldn't tell which way was up. Her lungs felt ready to burst, and for a second, she almost panicked. She'd escaped the surfboard, she realized frantically, but she was in danger of drowning.

Just as she thought she might never make it,

Nancy caught sight of the sky above her. The undercurrent tried to spin her over again, but she fought it and pulled herself up through the water until her head broke the surface. Gratefully Nancy filled her lungs with air, pushed her streaming hair out of her face, and looked around. Just a few feet away, her surfboard bobbed peacefully on the waves. Nancy swam over to it and climbed on, then spotted her sail. It was spread out on the water like a giant magenta scarf, and Nancy remembered that awful snap she'd felt when she'd turned the boom. What had happened? Those poles had to be sturdy, they couldn't just snap in two when the wind got strong. Or could they?

Off in the distance, Dirk Bowman was stretched out on his board, pulling himself against the current to reach Nancy. She waved to let him know she was okay, then caught hold of her sail and dragged it from the water. Hand over hand, she pulled the pole up. When she saw the end of it, where it had snapped, she shivered in spite of the hot sun beating down on her back.

There was a clean slice three quarters of the way through the pole and then a ragged edge where the wind had done the rest of the job. Someone had sawed partway through it, and Nancy shivered again, remembering Ricardo standing at the dock that morning, watching her climb into the boat.

Nancy raised her head and looked at Dirk, who was still bucking the waves to get to her. Maybe he and Ricardo knew each other. Why not? Their jobs brought them to the same beach every day, and maybe Dirk had mentioned that he was taking her windsurfing, so Ricardo had decided to try to get rid of her, making it look like an accident. Just like Kim, Nancy thought.

First the man-of-war, then the windsurfing incident. Ricardo wasn't exactly subtle with the messages he was sending her, and Nancy wondered how many more "accidents" she'd have to survive before she found out what he was involved in.

She was still staring at the pole, fingering the ragged edge, when she heard the buzz of a motor close by. Looking up, she saw a sleek raspberry-and-turquoise speedboat heading toward her. It zipped past, making choppy waves so that Nancy had to drop the pole and clutch the board with both hands. The driver made a sharp turn and then sped back, cutting the twin engines at the last possible second.

"Hi there!" the driver called out. She was a beautiful woman just a couple of years older than Nancy, with golden skin, silky blond hair, and a smile in her wide green eyes. "Need a lift?" she asked.

"It looks that way, doesn't it?" Nancy said, laughing. "I'm not really stranded though."

She pointed to Dirk. "But thanks for the offer."

The woman pulled her dark glasses down from the top of her head and peered through them at Dirk. "Oh, are you with him? Well, let me tell you, he's cute, but he's a klutz, if you know what I mean. I should know—I'm his boss." With a delightful smile, she stuck her hand over the side of the boat. "I'm Lila Templeton."

So she was the fun lady Dirk had mentioned. Shaking Lila's outstretched hand, Nancy glanced over her shoulder at Dirk, who was closer but still struggling with the waves. He lied to get me out here, she thought, and now it's time to pay him back. Laughing again, she hauled herself into Lila's boat. "I think I'll take you up on that offer after all," she said, "if you don't mind stopping at the island a moment so I can get my things."

Grinning, Lila Templeton started the engines, and the boat took off with a roar. As they passed Dirk, Lila slowed long enough to shout, "I want to talk to you the minute you get back!" She and Nancy made a fast stop at the island. Then Lila put the boat into high gear and sped off, leaving Dirk Bowman floundering in its wake.

As they sped back to the mainland, Lila kept up a steady stream of chatter about where Nancy should go and what she should do while she was in Florida. Mostly, though, she gave a sales pitch for her party to nowhere. "It's absolutely the wildest party you'll ever go to," she shouted. "You ought to try it while you're down here. You won't forget it, I promise you that!"

Nancy started to say that Dirk had already invited her, but she changed her mind. Lila seemed genuinely friendly, and Nancy didn't want to disappoint her. She was pretty sure she wouldn't have time for any wild island parties. She had other things to do, she thought grimly, and other people to see. Beginning with Ricardo.

"So what brings you to Lauderdale?" Lila asked, as they approached the docks. "Let me guess—spring break, right?"

"Right," Nancy said. She didn't like lying, but even though Lila seemed harmless and empty-headed, Nancy decided she shouldn't trust anyone. She'd talked to Dirk and look what had happened. Dirk had probably mentioned her to Ricardo, and it was just luck that her surfboard hadn't cracked open her skull half an hour ago.

When Lila docked the boat, Nancy thanked her for the ride and climbed out. "Don't forget the party, Nancy!" Lila called after her, and Nancy said she wouldn't. But she knew that that night she wouldn't be at any party.

Twenty minutes later, Nancy had grabbed a

bite to eat and was back on Fort Lauderdale Beach, looking for Ricardo. She had a strong urge to use one of George's most painful judo moves on him, but she knew that instead she would simply have to be patient. She would have to watch him, see where he went, whom he talked to. If she was careful, he just might lead her to Rosita.

The first place Nancy checked was Ricardo's lifeguard chair, but he wasn't in it. She strolled along the beach, keeping one eye out for Ricardo and the other out for stray men-of-war. Two of a kind, she thought with a grim smile.

Finally Nancy spotted the lifeguard standing ankle-deep in the surf. Beside him, holding his hand, was a blond girl in a red string bikini. It was Bess.

Nancy stopped, trying to figure out what to do. If Ricardo found out she and Bess were friends, he might decide that Bess should be the victim of a few accidents too. But if he thought that Bess was just another pretty girl out for a good time, he might relax with her. And Bess might learn something important about him. Nancy dropped back, trying to blend in with a group of sunbathers.

"Well, hi there, how's your foot?" a voice shouted. "I see you survived your encounter with the deadly man-of-war!"

Wishing he'd keep his voice down, Nancy

smiled at the boy who'd helped her up the day before. "Yes, I'm fine," she said softly.

"Great! I gotta hand it to you, you said you'd be back and here you are!" The boy didn't lower his voice a notch.

"Right," Nancy replied, watching as Ricardo turned his head and looked straight at her. Without a word to Bess, he dropped her hand and trotted down the beach, through the mass of sunbathing bodies, and out of sight. Here I am and there he goes, Nancy thought.

Bess looked at Nancy, her expression puzzled. Nancy waved goodbye to the boy and went to join Bess.

"Gosh," said Bess. "That was weird. That guy took one look at you and left."

Nancy started to explain that his name was Ricardo, and that he was the one she'd seen snooping around Kim's hotel room. But Bess was off on another subject.

"You're back awfully soon," she remarked. "Didn't your date with Dirk work out?"

"As a matter of fact, it was a real washout," Nancy admitted. "I shouldn't have gone with him. He didn't know a thing about the case."

"So now I guess he's through with you, right?" Bess said sarcastically. "Gee, maybe I still have a chance."

"Come on, Bess." Nancy sighed. "I'm sorry things got messed up for you, but you know I'm trying to find out what happened to Kim."

"Oh, and speaking of Kim," Bess said, "she still hasn't come to. While you were off with Dirk I was at the hospital. George is there now, but she has to leave in about an hour." Bess waded out of the water and onto the hard-packed sand. "Maybe you should go visit her. . . . So this Ricardo is really the same guy you saw in Kim's hotel room?"

Nancy nodded. "Don't take this the wrong way, Bess, but be careful around him, okay?"

"Okay," replied Bess, wide-eyed.

"All right. I'll see you around. I've got more investigating to do."

For a while, Nancy wandered along the beach, hoping she'd see Ricardo. But after an hour had gone by, she realized she was wasting her time. He probably wasn't on duty that day, and she knew he wouldn't put in an appearance unless he had to, not if he thought she was hanging around.

Nancy gave up and decided to go to the hospital. Maybe Kim would be awake by then. That would solve everything, she thought hopefully.

When she got to the hospital, Nancy saw Mrs. Baylor standing outside Kim's room, and for a moment, Nancy really was hopeful—Mrs. Baylor wasn't crying.

Keeping her fingers crossed, Nancy rushed down the hall. But as she got closer to Kim's mother she realized that if Mrs. Baylor wasn't crying, it was only because she was too shocked and frightened for tears.

"Mrs. Baylor?" Nancy was breathless, afraid of what she might hear. "Is Kim . . . is she . . . ?"

"She's worse," Mrs. Baylor whispered. "She's growing weaker, and the doctors are worried she might slip into a coma or . . ."

Or die, Nancy thought. And if that happens, then you'll be trying to solve more than a hit and run. It will be murder!

Chapter

Seven

IT WAS EARLY evening when Nancy let herself into her room at the Surfside Inn. She felt slightly guilty about leaving the hospital, but Mrs. Baylor had insisted. "You'll help Kim more by finding out why this happened to her," she'd said. And Nancy knew she was right; what she didn't know yet was how to solve the case. She had two leads—Ricardo and Rosita—and so far, she hadn't been able to follow either of them.

Maybe a shower will help clear your head, she thought, as she flicked on the lights. She stepped into the bathroom and was peeling off her clothes when she noticed the note stuck in the mirror.

Nan—I promised Bess I'd go with her on the party-to-nowhere boat, so that's where we are—nowhere! Bess still likes Dirk, which is why she insisted on going. She's also still ticked off at him for brushing her off and going out with you instead. But I know she understands that you have to do everything possible to solve the case.

George

Sighing, Nancy turned the shower on full blast and stepped into the warm spray. If all she had to worry about was Bess being mad at her, things would be great. Instead, things were about as rotten as they could be. She'd fallen for Dirk's line and spent an entire morning following a phony lead. And she'd really goofed with Ricardo. She should never have even hinted to him that she knew who he was. She'd probably be a lot closer to solving the case if she'd just kept her eyes open and her mouth shut.

With another sigh, Nancy stepped out of the shower and wrapped a towel around herself. She left the bathroom and stood in front of the window, staring out at the beach. Already, campfires were blazing here and there as groups of kids gathered for the next round of all-night parties. Nancy couldn't help thinking that she'd much rather be out there having fun than holed up alone in her hotel room. Then it hit her—if *she'd* rather be out somewhere, maybe Ricardo and Rosita would too. If not that night, then surely they'd been out on other nights.

She had Rosita's picture. And of the hundreds of kids on the beach and in the discos, there had to be at least one who'd seen her. It's worth a try, Nancy thought, as she put on a flashy sundress and her new sandals. After all, you said yesterday that if you had to, you'd walk up and down the beach asking anyone and everyone if they'd seen this girl. Well, now, it looks as if you have to.

It was eight o'clock by the time Nancy set out on her search. She was already on the beach when she realized she hadn't eaten anything since noon. There were plenty of fast-food places around. She could grab some food and ask a few questions at the same time.

Asking questions turned out to be easier than she'd anticipated. Halfway through a slice of pepperoni pizza, Nancy noticed that a cute boy in the next booth was paying more attention to her than to his pizza, which was getting cold, fast.

Nancy swallowed a bite of cheese, wiped her mouth, and raised her can of soda. That was all it took. In two seconds, the boy was sitting next to her. "Hi there," he said with a grin. "How you doing?"

"I'm not sure," Nancy replied, trying to look confused.

"What's the problem?"

"Oh, well, this is going to sound weird, but I was supposed to meet a friend of a friend when I got to Lauderdale," Nancy explained, making it up as she went along. "But I get here and what happens? I can't find her! She's not at the hotel, she's not on the beach, she's not anywhere."

"So?" The boy moved over in the booth and casually slid his arm across the back of it. "My name's Mike, by the way, and I don't think your story's weird at all. Your friend's friend is probably having a blast and just forgot about you. My advice is to enjoy yourself and forget about *her.*"

"Well, I would, except for one thing." Nancy noticed that Mike's hand was now resting on her bare shoulder. "I was supposed to give her something . . . some money. And I just know I can't have a good time until I find her and get that cash off my hands."

"Well, a good time's definitely what it's all about," Mike said, tightening his fingers on her shoulder. "Why don't you let me help you?"

"I was hoping you'd say that." Nancy

reached into her straw shoulder bag and took out the photo. "Here she is. Her name's Rosita."

"Pretty," Mike said, barely glancing at the picture. "But not as pretty as you."

"Thanks," Nancy replied, "but have you seen her?"

"Afraid not. Now, what are you and I going to do for fun tonight?" Mike scooted even closer to Nancy and bent his head down as if he were going to kiss her.

At the last second, Nancy ducked under his arms and left him sitting alone in the booth. Her plans for the night just didn't include Mike. "Sorry," she told him, "but until I find Rosita, I'm afraid I won't have any fun at all."

Abandoning her pizza, Nancy went out into the warm, breezy night, Mike frowning after her. From now on, she told herself, no more warm-up conversations. Just show the picture and ask the question. If you get stuck with any more Mikes, this search will take forever.

Unfortunately, Fort Lauderdale was full of Mikes, looking to have fun. Some were nice, some came on a little too strong, a few actually took her questions seriously. All of them were interested in Nancy, and none of them had seen Rosita.

By ten-thirty, Nancy was starting to feel discouraged. She'd hit every fast-food place on the strip and turned down invitations to dance in at least half the discos—and still no Rosita. What was the girl, anyway? A phantom? Somebody has to have seen her, Nancy thought.

By that time, the beach parties were going strong. Campfires were blazing, and radios and cassettes were blasting up and down the shoreline. Carrying her sandals, Nancy strolled along the soft, cool sand, stopping at every gathering to ask if anyone had seen the girl in the picture.

One girl thought she looked just like a girl from her dorm. "But she didn't come to Lauderdale, so it couldn't be the same one, could it?"

No, Nancy agreed, it couldn't. She was getting so many "sorrys," and "never saw hers," and "forget about her, stick with mes," that when she finally heard the words, "Oh, sure," she thought she'd imagined them.

"What did you say?" she asked the boy who'd spoken.

"I said, sure, I saw her about twenty minutes ago." He took a closer look at the photograph. "Yeah, that's the one. She was with one of the lifeguards. Ricardo, I think his name is."

Suddenly Nancy wasn't tired anymore. Her luck was changing. "Where were they?" she asked.

"Over that way," the boy said, pointing down the beach. "They were leaning against some trees, talking." He smiled and gave

Nancy a long look. "Hey, if you don't find them, come on back, why don't you? I plan to be here all night long."

"Thanks," Nancy replied, smiling, "but I don't." She trotted down the beach, keeping her fingers crossed that Ricardo and Rosita would still be there.

As Nancy approached a grove of palm trees she saw two shadowy figures emerge and begin walking along the wet sand, close to the water, toward the docks where Dirk had taken her that morning. The tide was still out, and the moon was full. Nancy could see clearly that one of the figures was Ricardo. The other one—shorter and with long, dark hair—had to be Rosita.

Nancy followed them, keeping a safe distance, sticking to the trees wherever there were any. Ricardo and Rosita seemed to be having a very intense conversation, and Nancy was sure they had no idea she was behind them. She was looking ahead, not really watching where she was going, when she stepped into another grove of palms, tripped over two reclining bodies and went sprawling head first into the sand.

A girl gave a piercing shriek and a boy grumbled, "Hey, give us a break, huh? Things were just getting romantic here!"

"Sorry, sorry," Nancy said, trying not to laugh. It would have been funny, but she was worried. Had Ricardo and Rosita heard the shriek? Not wanting to lose sight of them—or ruin the little love scene—Nancy stepped out of the trees and into the bright moonlight.

Ricardo and Rosita had stopped. They were looking in Nancy's direction. As soon as Ricardo saw her, he grabbed Rosita's hand, and the two of them took off running.

Nancy tore after them, not bothering to hide anymore. All she wanted was to catch up with them. Running on the wet, hard-packed sand, she saw them round a bend in the shoreline, and pushed herself even harder, not wanting to lose them. The music from the beach parties was growing fainter; as Nancy rounded the bend, she realized she'd left the crowds behind. She stopped suddenly and looked around, panting from her dash along the beach.

In front of her were the docks. She saw a few boats tied up and heard soft thuds as they bumped against the pilings. But that was all. Nancy was alone.

Still breathing hard, Nancy kicked at the sand in frustration. Then she headed for the docks, thinking that Ricardo and Rosita might be hiding in one of the boats. Of course, the way her luck was running, they'd probably doubled back. They could be sitting around a campfire at that very minute, she told herself, roasting hot dogs and having a good laugh.

Nancy had dropped her sandals somewhere along the way, and as she stepped onto the wooden pier, she reminded herself to be careful of splinters. But before she'd taken two steps, she gasped—not because she felt a splinter sliding into her foot, but because a hand, reaching out from the shadows, was closing tightly on her arm.

Chapter

Eight

NANCY WHIRLED AROUND, ready to fight as hard as she had to, and found herself facing the pretty, black-haired girl whose photograph she'd been carrying with her for the past four hours. Nancy glanced around nervously. No Ricardo in sight, but she figured he was lurking somewhere close by, watching.

Still on edge, Nancy looked at the girl again and was surprised to see that she was nervous too. Her eyes were wide with fear. She'd dropped Nancy's arm and was clenching her hands together tightly.

"Rosita," Nancy said. "You're Rosita, aren't you?"

69

The name turned the girl's fear to terror. She backed away and shook her head vehemently. "Maria," she stammered. "Maria."

Nancy was confused. For one thing, the girl whom she'd thought was her enemy was hardly acting like an enemy—one loud "boo" from Nancy and she'd probably collapse. Furthermore, her name wasn't Rosita.

"Okay," Nancy said. "You're Maria. My name's Nancy Drew. Now that the introduction's out of the way, why don't you tell me what you and Ricardo and Rosita are up to? Whatever you got Kim involved in just might have killed her, and . . ."

The girl was shaking her head again, holding out her hand for Nancy to stop talking. "Please," she said in Spanish, "I can explain everything, but I speak very little English."

Nancy nodded. "That's all right," she said, also in Spanish. "I know your language, so go ahead and explain. I'm listening."

Maria breathed a sigh of relief and began to talk.

Nancy *did* know Spanish, but after two sentences, she realized she didn't know Maria's Spanish. Still frightened, Maria was talking away a mile a minute, and she was speaking in a dialect that Nancy could hardly follow.

Nancy followed Maria's story as best she could, though, and did manage to learn that

Maria was an illegal alien. Her country was in the middle of a violent revolution and lots of people were escaping to the United States to start a new life. Kim had been hiding her in her hotel room.

"From the police?" Nancy asked. "Kim was hiding you from the immigration police?"

Maria shook her head and spoke rapidly again, saying something about the people she'd paid to bring her to Florida. "They were evil," she said. They didn't let her go, as they'd promised; they were going to make her work for them, for nothing, "like a slave." She was running from them, and Kim had helped her. Maria said something about Ricardo, but Nancy didn't understand. She decided to let Maria finish talking; then she'd ask questions.

Kim had made Maria promise to stay in the hotel room, but after many days, Maria had had to get out. She was followed and ran back to the hotel; someone broke in later while she was in the room, but she escaped.

That's how they found out about Kim, Nancy thought. But who were "they"? Kim definitely had been talking to Ricardo that morning on the phone, but why? He had to be one of the "evil ones," and Kim just didn't know it. She'd trusted him for some reason, and he'd double-crossed her.

"What about Ricardo?" Nancy asked. "What's he got to do with all this? And who

71

else is involved, Maria? Don't be afraid to tell me. I promise, I'll help you if I can."

Maria latched on to the name Ricardo and said a lot of things, none of which Nancy understood except that he had a bad temper. Nancy didn't need to be told that. "But what about the others?" she asked. "Ricardo can't be the only one. You talked about evil people. Who are the rest of them? Please tell me!"

Maria nodded eagerly. "One of them is—" She stopped in midsentence, her eyes widening in terror. "Oh, no!" she cried, pointing behind Nancy. "No!"

Nancy heard a scuffling sound in back of her and started to turn, but it was too late. Something hard—a rock? a club?—came crashing down on her head. She heard Maria scream, but it sounded muffled and distant. Then she saw the wooden slats of the dock as she fell. They were fuzzy because a dark mist was rising in front of her eyes. She blinked, but the mist kept rising; she tried to listen, but her ears were filled with a low roar, like highway traffic heard from far away. Finally the mist closed over her completely, and she couldn't see or hear anything at all.

When Nancy came to, the first thing she felt was pain. She hurt all over, but her head was the worst. She started to open her eyes, then shut them tightly, gasping at the pain. If only she could move her hand to the back of her head to rub it and ease some of the throbbing.

Something was stopping her, though; she wasn't sure what. She must have been lying on her arms, because they were tingling as if they'd been asleep. She tried to stretch one arm, then the other, to make the needles go away, but all she could move were her fingers.

Suddenly she became aware of another sensation—water. Her feet and legs were wet, and every few seconds, water splashed against her thighs. Had she fallen asleep on the beach?

Then she remembered. She'd been talking to Rosita. No, not Rosita. Maria. Maria had screamed, and then everything had gone black. Nancy hadn't fallen asleep, she'd been knocked out. And whoever had done it—she'd put her money on Ricardo—had dragged her onto the beach and left her there with the waves lapping at her legs. Funny, she'd always thought the sand would make a nice soft bed. So why did she feel as if she were lying on cement?

Time to get up, Nancy, she told herself. Forget the pain, just get up and go after him. She tried to stretch her arms again and suddenly realized that they were above her head. And she wasn't lying on soft sand, either. In fact, she wasn't lying at all. She was leaning against something very hard, something that had absolutely no give to it.

Nancy forced her eyes open and waited for her vision to clear. It was still night—pitch black—but if she craned her neck back, she could see the moon up above. She could also see where her hands were. They were up above too, tied over her head. No wonder her arms ached.

Nancy turned her head, scraping her cheek against something rough and cold. Then she felt the water wash against her thighs again, and realized that her feet were tied too. She peered down, trying to see where she was.

The night breeze was warm, but Nancy started shivering violently when she realized that she'd been tied, hand and foot, to one of the pier pilings, a rough, wooden pillar shooting straight out of the water. She was somewhere in the middle of it; if she tilted her head back far enough, she could just see the lip of the pier. But what made her shiver, what made her want to scream, was that she could also see the waterline on the piling. It was a foot above her head. Already the water was lapping against her thighs. Soon it would be at her waist, then at her shoulders. The tide was coming in, and Nancy was trapped in its path.

She heard a low, moaning sound and realized it was coming from her. Scream, she told herself. You got hit on the head, not in the throat. She tried to take a deep breath, and that's when she felt the gag in her mouth and the tape on her cheek. There was no way she could scream; the only sound she could make was a soft moan nobody would hear. She'd been tied, gagged, and left to drown.

Chapter

Nine

NANCY FOUGHT TO keep from panicking, but she lost the battle. She'd never been so trapped; the feelings of terror and helplessness were overwhelming. She was at the end of the pier, which was far enough out in the water to give her a tantalizing view of the bonfires around the bend in the beach. She could even see the shadows of the people around those bonfires, and every once in a while she heard shouts of laughter.

Frantically Nancy pulled and twisted against the ties that held her to the pier. She didn't know how long she kept it up, but when she finally stopped, she was limp with exhaustion and her skin was burning from being scraped against the piling. If she could have screamed, her throat would have been raw.

If they wanted to kill you, she thought tiredly, why didn't they just dump you in the middle of the ocean while you were still unconscious? Why put you through this kind of torture? They'd even tied her hands with the sash of her sundress. An extra-evil touch.

Evil. That's what Maria had called them, and she'd been right. For a moment, Nancy wondered what had happened to the frightened girl. Ricardo must have gotten her, she thought. Then, as the water washed up, hitting the middle of her back, Nancy began struggling and twisting again. But she was too tired and too sore to keep it up for very long. Sagging against the piling, she rubbed her forehead on the back of her wrist and closed her eyes.

Breathless, half-covered with water, Nancy thought of how she must look—like a huge barnacle in a dress. The thought made her want to laugh. You're getting hysterical, she warned herself. Her head was throbbing violently, and when she opened her eyes, she saw that the dark mist was closing in. If she passed out, she knew she'd never make it.

Nancy closed her eyes again, and that's

when she heard the footsteps on the pier. Looking up, she saw two faces bending over the edge, staring down at her. Nancy blinked, fighting back the mist, and realized that she recognized the faces. One belonged to the handsome "maintenance" man from Kim's hotel room; the other was the guy who'd delivered the flowers to the hospital. Not bothering to wonder what they were doing there, Nancy moaned as loudly as she could, begging them with her eyes to help her. The two faces lingered above her for a moment, then faded away like ghosts into the darkness.

Ghosts, Nancy thought. That's what they were. You're so far gone, you're hallucinating. She let her head drop and felt a wave splash high on her back, hitting her shoulder blades.

Then Nancy felt something else, something that made the dark mist evaporate—her feet were loose. Whatever they were tied with had stretched, and Nancy was almost able to uncross her ankles. If she could do that, she could get her feet free. What she'd do then, she wasn't sure, but she didn't care. One thing at a time, she told herself, and started to wiggle her feet, ignoring the scrapes on her knees and the ache in her arms.

It seemed to take forever, but finally Nancy did it. Her feet were side by side and she was able to slip one and then the other out of the binding. Her arms felt as if they were going to rip out at the shoulders, and she managed to wrap her legs around the piling. Then what?

The water lapped at her neck, and Nancy instinctively gripped the piling with her knees and tried to push herself up. The sash binding her hands moved up too, just a fraction. That's it, Nancy told herself. You've climbed enough trees, now shinny up this pole.

Inch by inch, Nancy pushed herself up the piling. The tide kept coming in, and she must have swallowed half the ocean, but finally her head was above the waterline, and even though she was still trapped, she knew she was going to make it.

She couldn't use her teeth on the sash, but when she saw that the cloth wasn't completely soaked, Nancy began to scrape it up and down on a corner of the piling. At last she felt the cloth begin to give. With a final burst of strength, Nancy pulled her hands free, shinnied the rest of the way up the piling, and hauled herself onto the pier.

The first thing she did was rip the gag from her mouth. Then she lay still, gasping and listening to the water swirl below her. She told herself to get moving, but her body wouldn't budge. Her mind was working, though, and when she thought of Maria, she was finally able to sit up. For all Nancy knew, Maria was dead. No, Maria had said something about being made to work like a slave. Whoever wanted her, wanted her alive, and Ricardo must have taken her to that person.

Ricardo. Nancy had to find him, not just for Maria's sake, but for her own. She had a personal score to settle with him. But she wasn't going to do it on her own, not again. She wanted the police backing her up the next time. It was safer, and besides, she'd need them to keep her from setting fire to Ricardo's chair while he was in it.

Nancy felt the adrenaline pumping as she pushed herself to her feet and stumbled away from the pier. She even managed to trot a little as she rounded the bend in the beach and came within sight of the all-night partiers. The bonfires were still glowing, but not so brightly, and the radios and cassette recorders were playing softer music. It was getting late. No, it was getting early, Nancy reminded herself; morning couldn't be far away.

As soon as she reached the main beach, Nancy headed for the street, looking for a public phone. She'd thought of calling from her hotel and then cleaning up while she waited for the police, but she wanted them to see her first. She knew she looked like the survivor of a shipwreck, and if the police saw what Ricardo had done, they'd work that much harder.

When she was halfway down the beach, she spotted a string of phone booths. The adrenaline wasn't pumping so hard by then, and she felt exhausted, as if she were trekking across a desert, and the phone booth was her oasis.

Nancy had almost reached the booth when a scream rang out. At first she took it to be a good-natured, party-type scream, but then she heard other screams and saw people running toward the water. The tide had washed something ashore. What was it? A shark? A jellyfish?

"It's a body!" a boy shouted, rushing by Nancy. "It's a *body!*"

Maria, Nancy thought instantly. Maria put up too big a fight, and Ricardo or whoever he worked with killed her. Forgetting about the police for the moment, Nancy joined the rest of the crowd heading toward the water. She didn't want to see a dead body, but she had to find out if it was Maria.

There must have been a hundred people gathered around, and Nancy had to push through them until she was able to see. Someone had thrown a large beach towel over the body. Nancy broke free of the crowd and moved quickly to the towel, wanting to get it over with.

"Poor guy," a voice said, and Nancy stopped.

"Yeah," someone else said. "Drowning— what a way for a lifeguard to go, huh?"

"Lifeguard?" Nancy asked.

"Yeah." A boy nodded grimly. "What was his name? Ricardo, that's it. Ricardo."

Chapter

Ten

Nancy stepped back from the towel-draped body. "Are you sure it's Ricardo?" she asked.

"Hey, I helped pull him out of the water," the boy replied. "And I've talked to him every day since I've been here. I know what he looks like." The boy paused. "Hey, you look sick. Were you a friend of his?" he asked.

Nancy shook her head. "No, but I knew who he was."

"Yeah, well, it's too bad, huh? And you want to know something? He didn't drown—he was shot." The boy held up his hand. "And, yes,

I'm sure. I pulled him out of the water, remember?"

Stunned, Nancy pushed her way through the crowd and stumbled back up the beach, trying to figure out what had happened. Why had Ricardo been shot? Had he lost Maria, and had the people he worked with killed him for it?

When she reached the street, Nancy heard the wail of a siren in the distance. The police, coming to investigate Ricardo's murder. She knew she should talk to them, but what would she say? The last time she saw him, he was with a girl named Maria, but she had no idea where Maria was. She had no idea who Ricardo worked for or who killed him. You don't really know anything at all, Nancy told herself. Your main suspect is dead, and you're back to square one.

The Surfside Inn was just across the street, and Nancy decided to go there first, to shower and change. Then she'd return to the beach and talk to the police. But after she got the key from the desk and let herself into the room, Nancy realized she was too tired to take a shower. She was so wiped out, she was actually staggering. Her eyes were playing tricks on her, too. Instead of two single beds, she saw four, then two, then four again. Stumbling across the room, she bumped into the cot that Bess used, fell onto it, and was asleep before her head hit the pillow.

"Look at this!" a voice was saying. "There's a body on my cot!"

Nancy burrowed her face deeper into the crook of her elbow. "Go away," she mumbled.

Another voice said, "Look, she didn't even bother to change. How's that for lazy?"

"Please," Nancy groaned, "not so loud." She yawned and tried to slip back into sleep, but someone sat down on the cot, making it jiggle back and forth.

"Hey, Nan," Bess said, laughing, "I don't mind if you sleep here, but don't you think you'd be more comfortable without my make-up kit poking you in the neck?"

Nancy moaned and shook her head, but it was too late—she was awake. She opened one eye and peered up through her tangled hair. Bess and George were staring down at her, looking extremely amused. "What's happening?" she asked.

"Why don't *you* tell *us?*" George suggested.

"Yeah," Bess said, grinning. "We thought we had a wild night, but it looks like yours was wilder. Couldn't even bother to take off your clothes before you fell asleep, huh?"

"Wild night?" Nancy croaked. Her throat was bone dry, and her tongue felt too big for

85

her mouth. Swallowing, she pushed herself up on her elbows and turned onto her back. "It was wild, all right."

When Bess and George saw how scratched and bruised she was, their teasing grins disappeared and their mouths dropped open.

"Nan, what *happened* to you?" Bess cried in horror.

"That must have been some battle," George said. "Are you okay?"

"I will be, once I shower and eat and drink about a gallon of water." Nancy sat up slowly and rubbed her neck. "You're right, George," she remarked, "it was some battle."

"Well, tell us!" Bess demanded.

George went to the vending machine in the hall and brought back a soda and a package of peanut butter crackers. Nancy ate first, then told them everything that had happened the night before.

"We heard about Ricardo when we got in," Bess told her. "That's all anybody's talking about on the beach."

"It looks like he wasn't a bad guy after all," George said.

"What do you mean?"

"Well, he was an illegal himself."

Hmm, thought Nancy. Just like Maria.

"Yeah," Bess said, "the police tried to check up on him and found out he'd been working with a fake green card ever since he reached

Florida. And it seems that a lot of people around here knew about it."

George nodded. "One of the other lifeguards told me that Ricardo tried to help other illegals—you know, get them cards and find them work, stuff like that."

"So he must have been helping Maria all along," Nancy said. That explained why he'd smiled when Kim got hit, she thought. It was a smile of anger—he'd been challenged and he was ready to fight. "But why did he have it in for me?" she wondered aloud, remembering the satisfied look on his face when she'd stepped on the man-of-war.

"Why shouldn't he? He didn't know who you were," Bess pointed out. "Kim didn't know you were coming down, and she probably never even mentioned you. He probably thought you were going to turn him over to the authorities or something."

"Right," Nancy agreed. "He didn't trust anyone." She ran her fingers through her hair and sighed. "Boy, I'm really stuck now. I don't have the vaguest idea what to do next."

Bess took Nancy's hand and pulled her off the bed. "Take a shower and then put something in your stomach besides soda and crackers," she told her. "Once you feel human again, you'll be able to think."

Nancy couldn't help noticing that Bess was back to her old friendly self. Dirk must have made all the right moves, she thought. Then she thought of something else. "Kim!" she cried. "I completely forgot!" She quickly told Bess and George about Kim's condition while she dialed the hospital room. The line was busy.

Ten minutes and three calls later, it was still busy.

"Look," George said, "go shower. We'll keep trying the hospital. Anyway, who knows? Kim might have recovered. She could be running up a long distance phone bill right now."

"Let's hope so," Nancy said, and headed for the shower. Even though the sharp spray stung every cut and scratch, the water felt wonderful, and Nancy thought she might never come out. She was soaping her hair for the second time when Bess walked in.

"Nan?" she called. "I just wanted to apologize for the way I acted about Dirk. I was really mad at him, not at you. I hope you know that."

"It's okay," Nancy called back, over the hiss of the water. Then she poked her head out of the shower curtain and grinned. "I take it you two got together again last night?"

"We sure did!" Bess ran a brush through her hair and laughed. "He's absolutely incredible!"

"Well, I'm glad somebody had fun," Nancy joked. "Did you meet Lila Templeton?"

Bess nodded. "She was really nice. She asked why you weren't there, but I just said something had come up."

"That's for sure!" Nancy ducked back in the shower and started rinsing her hair.

"I wouldn't mind being in Lila's shoes," Bess went on with a giggle. "Everybody who works for her is tan, male, and gorgeous! And when they drop the partiers off at the island, she gets to take off in that boat with ten beautiful men!"

Nancy laughed and poured some conditioner on her hair. "Sounds great!"

"It is," Bess agreed, "but I'm starting to feel a little guilty."

"Guilty? What for?"

"Well, I mean, there we were, cruising along in the *Rosita,* having a terrific time, while you were tied to that piling, fighting for your life, and—"

"The what?" Nancy turned the water off and stuck her head out again. "What did you say?"

"I said I was feeling a little guilty about having such a good time when—"

"I heard that part," Nancy interrupted. "You said you were cruising along in the . . . the what?"

"The boat," Bess said, looking confused. "Lila Templeton's boat—the *Rosita.*"

89

Chapter

Eleven

I MISSED IT!" Nancy said. "I completely missed it!" She stepped into her new yellow drawstring shorts, pulled on a stretchy, yellow-striped tank top, and reached for the blow-dryer. "Kim said, 'The . . . it was . . . Rosita.' I kept thinking she meant a girl, and all the time she meant a boat!"

"You really think Lila Templeton brings people in illegally?" Bess asked.

"I think she does more than that," Nancy said over the whine of the blow-dryer. "I think she brings them in, takes their money, and then ships them off to her family's orange groves to work for nothing."

"Cheap labor," George remarked.

"The cheapest," Nancy agreed. "No wonder she's got so much money. No wonder the *Rosita* is just a big water toy to her. Except it isn't really a toy," she added. "It's a perfect front for what she's doing."

"You mean while everybody's partying on the island," Bess said, "Lila takes the boat, picks up the immigrants, and hides them somewhere on the boat until she gets back to Fort Lauderdale?"

"Why not?" George asked. "The *Rosita*'s big enough."

Nancy turned off the dryer. "I don't think it's just Lila, though," she said. "Remember the guys I told you about—the 'maintenance' man and the one who dropped off the flowers at the hospital? When I was out on that pier, I thought I'd imagined them. But now I'm positive they were there."

"You think they work for Lila," George said.

"Right. It makes sense, doesn't it?" Nancy asked. "That maintenance guy was as phony as a three-dollar bill; I just didn't know what he was doing there. But he was probably checking the room to make sure there wasn't any evidence against Lila. And the florist guy must have been checking to make sure Kim wasn't spilling the beans."

"I'll bet they followed you around last

night," George told her. "And you led them right to Maria and Ricardo."

Nancy nodded. "Lila's got a whole fleet of gorgeous men doing her dirty work." Her feet still sore, she limped over to the cot and, wincing, slipped on a pair of thongs. The sandals she'd worn the night before were lost forever on the beach. "And, Bess," she said, "remember what happened when you first introduced me to Dirk?"

"How could I forget? He practically tripped over his own feet to stand next to you." Bess rolled her eyes and shook her head. "The minute he met you, it was like I didn't exist."

"Not the minute he met me," Nancy reminded her. "It was the minute I started talking about Kim."

"That's right," George said. "He said he was 'sort of a mystery nut' and he'd like to help you."

Bess shook her head again. "What a line!"

"Yeah, but he wasn't using that line because he was interested in me," Nancy said. "The only one he was interested in was Kim, and that's because—"

"Because he works for Lila Templeton," Bess finished with a groan. "How come I always fall for the wrong guy?" she asked, plopping down on one of the beds. "This time I really, really thought I'd found somebody special, and he turns out to be a creep, *the* creep!"

Nancy couldn't help laughing. "Don't feel too bad, Bess. I fell for him, too." Grinning, she told them about the broken pole on her windsurfing sail. "I mean I really fell for him!"

"Well, now that we've got it all figured out," George said, "what are we going to do about it?"

"Good question," Bess remarked. "The only one who can prove anything is Maria, and who knows where she is?"

"Kim could prove it," Nancy said, "if she's still . . ." Instead of finishing the awful thought, Nancy reached for the phone and dialed Kim's hospital room. "Now there's no answer at all," she reported.

"What could that mean?" Bess asked.

"I don't know." Nancy suddenly jumped up and headed for the door. "Come on, let's get to the hospital and find out."

Half an hour later, Nancy, Bess, and George were standing nervously outside the door to Kim's hospital room. They looked at each other for a moment; then Nancy took a deep breath and pushed it open.

Kim was gone.

The bed was empty and freshly made, ready for a new patient. The only reminders of Kim were two flower arrangements—one was dried and drooping, but the second looked as if it had just been delivered.

Bess's eyes filled with tears. "We're too late," she whispered.

George bit her lip. "I can't believe she's—"

"Wait a minute," Nancy broke in. "This doesn't have to mean she's dead. Maybe they moved her to a different room or took her for tests or X rays or something. Come on!"

The three friends dashed out of the room and headed down the hall. As they turned a corner they heard a loud commotion at the nurses' station.

"I never authorized any such thing!" a voice cried. "How could you possibly think I would?"

It was Kim's mother, but she didn't look grief-stricken. She looked furious.

"Mrs. Baylor?" Nancy rushed up to her. "What's going on?"

"I'd like to know myself!" Mrs. Baylor exclaimed. "I leave my daughter's room for all of twenty minutes to get a cup of coffee in the cafeteria and what do I find when I come back? An empty bed, that's what I find. With no daughter in it!"

"I'm sorry, Mrs. Baylor," the nurse said nervously. "But the doctor who signed her out said you wanted her taken back to River Heights as soon as possible."

"That's ridiculous! Why would I have her moved at such a crucial time?"

"You mean Kim had gotten even worse?" Nancy asked.

"No, she was getting better! Just a couple of hours ago, she actually woke up," Mrs. Baylor explained. "She didn't say anything, of course, she was too weak. But she knew who I was—she smiled at me before she went back to sleep. The doctors said it would be just a matter of days before she'd be back on her feet." She turned to the nurse again. "They also told me it was very important to keep her quiet and calm," she said accusingly. "It would be the most ridiculous thing in the world for me to take her back to River Heights right now!"

The nurse started to say something, but Mrs. Baylor didn't give her a chance. "I'm going to see your supervisor right this minute," she told her. "And you'd better hope she has some answers for me! If she doesn't, heads are going to roll around here!" Without a backward glance, Mrs. Baylor strode to the elevator and furiously punched the button.

When she was gone, the red-faced nurse puffed out about a gallon of air. "This is definitely not my day," she complained. "I'm new here and all I did was follow a doctor's orders, and now my job's on the line!"

Nancy barely heard her. "If we'd just gotten

here an hour ago, this whole thing would never have happened," she muttered.

"What are you talking about?" Bess asked.

"Those flowers," Nancy said, pacing back and forth in front of the desk.

"What flowers?"

"In Kim's room, remember? One of the bouquets was drooping and the other was fresh. I'll bet you a brand-new string bikini that they were both sent by the same person."

"Lila?" George asked.

"Lila." Nancy stopped pacing and shook her head. "Lila Templeton has been one step ahead of me ever since I got here. That tan hunk who works for her probably delivered those flowers so he could find out what shape Kim was in. When he realized she was recovering, he called Lila. That's why the phone was busy. And Lila decided that Kim better disappear."

Nancy thought for a moment, then suddenly turned to the nurse. "That doctor," she said, "the one who signed Kim Baylor out. Who was he?"

"It wasn't a he, honey," the nurse replied. "That doctor was a she, and she had two of the cutest orderlies with her that I ever saw in my life."

"Lila Templeton," Nancy said again. "The doctor had blond hair, right?" she asked.

"Blond hair and big green eyes," the nurse replied. "She was real friendly, smiled a lot."

"A great bedside manner, huh?" Nancy asked with a wry smile. Without waiting for an answer, she looked at Bess and George. "We've got to get going," she said.

"Where?" Bess wanted to know.

"To the *Rosita*."

"You think Lila has Kim on her boat?" George asked.

"Kim *and* Maria," Nancy said. "It makes sense, doesn't it? They're the only two people who can point a finger at Lila. She knows she has to get rid of them, and the *Rosita* is a perfect way to do it."

Bess's face turned pale under its tan. "You mean she'll kill them and dump them in the ocean?"

Nancy nodded. "Don't forget Ricardo," she said. "Lila Templeton has killed before, and unless we stop her, she's going to kill again."

Chapter

Twelve

AT SEVEN-THIRTY that night, the *Rosita* sat peacefully at the dock, swaying slightly in the breeze. It was a beautiful boat, sleek and trim, but with enough deck space for close to fifty people to dance on. Its rails were strung with brightly colored lights, and from somewhere on board, powerful speakers blasted rock music into the evening air. It was scheduled to leave at eight o'clock, and already the decks were filling with laughing, joking people, eager to party the night away.

As Nancy, Bess, and George joined a crowd of kids heading for the gangplank, Nancy raised her eyes and scanned the crew on the small upper deck. "I just spotted my friend the maintenance man," she whispered. "The florist is up there, too."

"And there's Dirk the Jerk," Bess hissed. "Is it my imagination, or does he look nervous?"

Dirk Bowman, wearing white cotton shorts and a muscle-hugging T-shirt, was standing at the rail, his eyes roving over the approaching partiers.

"I'd be nervous too," George said, "if I had Kim and Maria hidden away in the hold somewhere."

"Lila probably ordered them all to keep an eye out for me," Nancy said.

"But she thinks you're dead," Bess reminded her.

"She can't be sure," Nancy told her. "If she sent one of her goons to check, all he would have found is the sash from my sundress. Until she hears about my body being washed ashore, she can't take any chances."

"*We're* the ones taking a chance right now," George remarked. "If Dirk spots the three of us together, he's going to see right through our 'disguises.'"

Nancy nodded. She wished they really could have disguised themselves, but after all, they had to wear clothes that were right for a party to nowhere. George had on a long striped caftan with a hood that covered her hair and shadowed her face. Bess, whose figure was a dead giveaway, especially to Dirk, had reluctantly decided on a pair of baggy cotton pants, rolled to the knees and topped with an oversized shirt patterned with gaudy palm trees. "I look like a tourist," she'd complained, tucking her blond hair under a wide-brimmed straw hat.

Nancy was wearing a caftan too, but it didn't have a hood. She'd wrapped her hair in a bright paisley scarf, like a turban, and put on so much makeup that her face itched and her eyelids felt weighted down. She knew she and her friends looked completely different, but she also knew they had to be careful. "You're right," she said to George, "we'd better split up. As soon as the *Rosita* gets going, we can meet somewhere—how about the bow?—and start looking for Kim and Maria."

The minute the three friends parted, Nancy felt a hand on her arm. "Hey," a voice said in her ear, "want some company?"

Nancy turned and found herself looking into the brown eyes of a boy wearing a fish-net shirt, a gold neck chain, and a self-satisfied grin that didn't attract her at all, but she smiled at him anyway. "I sure do," she said softly. "I don't know anybody at all, and I was starting to feel a little lonely."

"Well, now you don't have to, because you know me. And I have a feeling that before the night's over, we'll be real close friends." He squeezed her hand and grinned again.

Nancy forced herself to laugh, and as they walked up the gangplank she glanced over her shoulder. George, tall and mysterious-looking in her hooded caftan, was in deep conversation with two guys, and Bess had attached herself to a group of giggling, dateless girls. She must be miserable, Nancy thought, smiling to herself.

"Welcome!" a sultry voice called out. "Welcome aboard the *Rosita!*"

It was Lila Templeton, dressed in a long robe of shimmering sea green silk that opened in the front to reveal an extremely small bikini. Her honey blond hair spilled over her bare shoulders like a lion's mane, and she was flashing her toothpaste-ad smile to everyone coming up the gangplank. "If there's anything my boys or I can do for you, just let us know," she called out, "because we want each and every one of you to have the most fantastic night of your lives!"

Each and every one of us except two, Nancy said to herself, thinking of Kim and Maria. Turning to her "date," she flashed a smile of her own, ducking her head and pretending to be fascinated with whatever he was babbling about. That got her safely past Lila, but she knew she'd still have to be careful of Lila's "boys," who were patrolling the deck like sentries.

Fortunately, the party to nowhere was booked solid, and Nancy soon found herself on the jam-packed deck, trying to dance and make conversation with her new friend, whose name she still didn't know. She was hot and sweaty, and she'd lost sight of Bess and George, but at least she was inconspicuous.

At eight o'clock, a cheer went up as the *Rosita* pulled smoothly away from the dock. In twenty minutes, they'd left the lights of Fort Lauderdale behind and were moving swiftly through the water under a starlit sky. Nancy decided she'd better start exploring. It wouldn't take long to reach the island, and she knew she had to find Kim and Maria before then, or it might be too late.

"Listen," she said when there was a break in the music, "I'm going to collapse if I don't get some breathing space. I think I'll just wander around a little bit, okay?"

"Aww, come on," her date said, "the party's just getting started." Grabbing her hand, he pulled Nancy close to him as a slow number began playing. "I thought you and I were going to spend the whole night together," he whispered in her ear.

"You thought wrong," Nancy whispered back. She slipped down out of the circle of his arms and turned him around until he was facing another girl. "Sorry, but I'm sure you won't have any trouble finding a partner."

Obviously not heartbroken, the boy immediately asked the other girl if she wanted to dance, and Nancy left them together, threading her way quickly through the crowd until she reached the deck rail. Then she craned her neck around, trying to find Bess and George.

She spotted George standing near the entrance to the galley, which was roped off, sipping a can of soda and watching the dancers. Bess was still attached to the group of unattached girls, tapping her foot to the music and looking frustrated. Lila was nowhere to be seen, but her boys were all over the place, carrying trays of drinks, mingling with the crowd, and keeping their eyes wide open, Nancy noticed.

Casually Nancy raised her hands above her head, as if she were stretching. Bess and George both caught the movement, and just as casually, started making their way toward the *Rosita*'s bow. Nancy lowered her hands, pretending to be adjusting her turban, but instead of the silk of the scarf, her hands came down on her hair.

What had happened to her scarf? Nancy's reddish blond hair was as big a clue to her identity as a fabulous figure was to Bess's. With her telltale hair swirling around her shoulders and her thick makeup dissolving in sweat, Nancy knew she'd be recognized by anyone who'd spent even five minutes with her. And that includes Lila, Dirk, and at least two more of Lila's boys, she thought frantically.

Nancy realized it was too late to go searching for her scarf. It must have come loose when she broke free from her date's arms, and had probably already been trampled by at least eighty feet. She grabbed her hair in both hands and swept it back, tying it in a loose knot that she knew wouldn't hold for long, but it was the best she could do. Hoping to get lost in the crowd, she moved into the mass of dancing bodies, and that's when she saw Lila's "maintenance" man.

He was heading straight toward Nancy, one hand in his pocket and both eyes on her face.

Whirling around, Nancy grabbed the hands of the nearest boy, not caring if he was with anyone else or not, and started dancing with him. When she sensed that the maintenance man was drawing close to her, she spun around again so that her back was to him. By that time, she'd lost her dance partner, but it didn't matter. What mattered was that the maintenance man had recognized her. She was sure of it. Just keep dancing, she told herself; at least it's rock and you can move fast.

With a few quick dance steps, Nancy reached the other side of the *Rosita*. Only then did she dare look back. She expected to spot the maintenance man somewhere in the crowd, but she found that was impossible. There were too many people bouncing, clapping, and swirling around the deck.

Nancy took a deep breath, tightened the knot in her hair, and headed toward the bow. The water was becoming rougher, and she clung to the rail, bumping into a few romantic couples on the way, but finally she reached the bow.

The deck was narrow there, and in spite of the lights on the rail, it was dark. Nancy stepped into the shadows, expecting to find Bess and George waiting for her.

No one was there. Nancy edged her way around the bow, toward the other side of the boat, but before she reached it, a voice—throaty and sultry—called out, "Looking for someone, Miss Drew?"

Chapter

Thirteen

TURNING SLOWLY, NANCY found herself face-to-face with Lila Templeton, her silk robe billowing gently in the breeze, her green eyes glittering as brightly as the barrel of the gun she held in her hand.

"I said," Lila repeated, "are you looking for someone?"

Nancy didn't bother to answer. "I have a question too," she said, keeping her eyes on the gun. "Is that the same gun that killed Ricardo?"

Lila laughed softly. "I'm afraid I don't know what you're talking about, but I suggest that you be careful, or it just might kill *you*. I also suggest that you be cooperative," she went on. "I want you to turn around and walk slowly and calmly back to the main deck."

"Then what?" Nancy asked.

"I guess you don't understand," Lila told her, stepping so close to Nancy that she felt the gun barrel pressing against her stomach. "I'm in charge. You don't ask questions, you don't make comments. You just do what I tell you. Now move!"

Nancy turned, raised her hands above her head and started walking. Behind her, Lila hissed, "Put your hands down!" and when Nancy felt the gun prodding her in the back, she decided not to push Lila any further. She lowered her arms and walked slowly around the bow, heading back to the main deck.

The music and laughter were still going strong, and for a second Nancy was tempted to break away and try to lose herself in the dancing crowd. But then what? she wondered. It wouldn't get her any closer to Kim and Maria, or to Bess and George, wherever they were. If she let Lila call the shots for a while, she might learn something. Besides, with a gun at her back, she figured she didn't have much choice.

"The galley," Lila ordered.

"I thought it would be off limits," Nancy quipped, figuring that that might be where Kim and Maria were hidden.

107

Lila laughed again. "Not for you, Miss Drew. Consider the *Rosita* your home. The last home you'll ever have."

With the gun barrel nestled between her shoulder blades, Nancy went down the steps and into the narrow galley. But Lila didn't stop there. She urged Nancy through it and past some bunk beds. At last Nancy stopped, thinking there was nowhere else to go.

But Lila shoved her roughly aside and, still aiming the gun at Nancy, dropped to her knees, took hold of a brass ring on the floor, and pulled up a section of the floor. Looking down, Nancy saw a steep metal staircase leading to the bottom of the boat.

"After you," Lila said.

Nancy lowered herself through the hole, found her footing, and stepped backward down the staircase. When she reached the bottom, she looked up, hoping that Lila would back down too, so she could grab her ankle and get the gun. But Lila came down facing forward, holding the gun in front of her, aimed at Nancy's chest.

They were in a very narrow, dimly lit passageway, with two doors on each side. Obviously not first-class accommodations, Nancy thought. "Look, I know all about your operation," she said to Lila. "I know you bring in illegal aliens, and then force them to work on your family's farms. They don't have any ID cards, not even fake ones, and they don't have any money, because you charged them so much to bring them into the country. If they escape you, they get caught by the immigration police. They're trapped."

"That's right," Lila agreed. "They're trapped, and so are you."

"Then you admit it?" Nancy asked.

Lila shrugged. "Why not? You're not going to tell anyone. In a few hours, you'll be food for the fish." Reaching into her pocket, she pulled out a key and slid it into the lock on one of the doors.

"One of my boys will be down soon to take care of you," she said, opening the right-hand door. "Until then, I suggest you and your friends enjoy the time you have left."

My friends? Nancy barely had time to wonder whether she meant Kim and Maria or Bess and George, before Lila shoved her inside and slammed the door shut.

"Nan!" Bess raced across the small, stuffy room and hugged her friend. "Thank goodness you're okay!" She pulled Nancy farther into the room. "Come on, join the party!"

Nancy looked around the dim room and couldn't help smiling. *All* her friends were there. George, Kim, and Maria were sitting on storage crates, a single can of soda on the floor

109

in front of them. With a slight grin, George pointed to it. "We've been passing it around," she said. "Help yourself."

Nancy shook her head. "Some party," she joked.

Everyone laughed, and the tension was broken for a moment. Then Nancy crossed the room and looked closely at Kim, who was wearing Bess's baggy pants and print shirt. Bess, she noticed, looked much more comfortable since she had stripped down to the bikini she'd brought along—for fun on the island. "Are you all right?" Nancy asked Kim gently.

"Physically, I'm okay, except for this," Kim replied quietly, holding up her plaster-casted arm. "Mentally, I'm terrified."

"That makes two of us," Nancy admitted. The room was incredibly hot, so she slipped out of her caftan, and instructed George to do the same. If they ended up in the water, Nancy didn't want them bogged down by unnecessary clothing. Feeling slightly cooler in her bikini, she sat down on a crate and took a sip of the soda. "Kim, why didn't you tell me what was going on when I came to your room the other day?"

"I didn't think there was time," Kim said. "I was freaking out—Maria was gone, and Ricardo was yelling at me to meet him. I just panicked."

Nancy nodded. "Did George and Bess tell you what happened to Ricardo?"

Kim took a deep breath and lowered her eyes. "Yes," she said softly. "I still can't believe it. I feel terrible about it. We weren't in love," she admitted with a sigh, "but he was special."

"How did you get involved in all this?" Bess asked.

"By the time Maria escaped from Lila, Ricardo and I were good friends," Kim explained. "He'd told me all about himself —how he tried to help illegals—and he knew I was sympathetic. So when Maria needed a place to stay, I was the obvious one to ask."

"How come you didn't go to the police?" George asked.

"I wanted to," Kim told her. "I knew Ricardo couldn't because he was an illegal too, but there was nothing to stop me. He didn't trust the police, though. He asked me to wait, and I did. But I should have gone anyway."

Maria, who had been quiet until then, brushed her long hair back from her face and spoke rapidly in Spanish.

Kim nodded. "Maria wants me to tell you that she'd tried to get Ricardo to talk to you. I'd told Maria about you when she was hiding out in my hotel room. I guess I said something about having a friend who was a detective and wishing you were here," Kim said with a smile. "But Ricardo wouldn't listen to her. He just didn't trust anyone. He didn't let her talk to you until last night."

"We really can't blame him for that," Nancy said softly.

"I don't think we should be talking about blame at all," Bess pointed out. "I think we should be talking about how to get out of here."

Nancy laughed. "You're right. It's a good thing the five of us are here, too, because we need all the brainpower we can get to figure this one out."

Springing to her feet, Nancy started exploring the room, which took her all of two minutes. "There's not even a closet to hide in," she remarked. "Not that hiding would do us any good."

"How about the crates?" George said. "Is there something we could do with them—hide in them, block the door with them?"

"I was thinking the same thing," Nancy said.

"They'd find us anyway," Bess told her. "I mean, nobody but Lila and her crew knows we're in here. So what if we blocked the door? They'd just wait until everybody's partying on the island and then break it down. We're trapped!"

Nancy knew that Bess was right. Hiding or

blocking the door would only postpone whatever was going to happen. It was a stopgap, and they needed an escape hatch. But Lila had made certain they didn't have one. She'd backed them into a corner, and she was closing in fast.

Suddenly Nancy felt a change in the rhythm of the *Rosita;* it seemed to slow down. The five girls steadied themselves as the boat began rocking from side to side.

"What's happening?" Kim asked.

"We've almost reached the island," George said. "The *Rosita's* too big to go all the way to shore, so they take everybody in on little speedboats. We'll be stopping any minute."

"And after everybody's ashore, the *Rosita* sails away," Bess continued. "With us on it."

"Yeah," Nancy said with a grim smile. "Then Lila's private party begins."

The girls looked at each other fearfully; they knew what was going to happen, but they didn't know how to stop it. At that moment, the door handle clicked. Everyone jumped, and then Bess gasped.

Standing in the open doorway was Dirk Bowman, a dimpled smile on his face and a shiny revolver in his hand.

Chapter

Fourteen

IN A FLASH, Bess darted across the room, stopping just a couple of feet in front of Dirk.

"Listen to me, Dirk! Please listen!" she cried. "I know what you think, but it's not true, it's really not! I don't know what's going on here. I don't know *anything,* and even if I did I wouldn't tell. You have to believe me!"

"Wait a minute," Dirk said, frowning. "I—"

"There's no time to wait!" Bess interrupted frantically. "I know what Lila plans to do with us, and you have to get me out of here. Please, Dirk, I'll do anything you want, I'll say anything you want, if you'll just let me go!"

As the other four listened in amazement, Bess kept on pleading with Dirk Bowman to save her. Kim and Maria stared at her in horror; obviously, they thought she was so panicked that she was willing to say anything to save her own neck.

Nancy was amazed too, but for a different reason: She knew that Bess was acting—and it was working. Dirk couldn't get a word in edgewise; he'd try to say something, but Bess would immediately interrupt him, pleading, whining, shouting, whispering, doing anything to distract him. From the look on George's face, Nancy could tell that she hadn't been fooled either. If the situation hadn't been so serious, the two of them might have started clapping. It was a beautiful performance, and it was up to Nancy to take advantage of it.

Slowly but smoothly, Nancy moved closer to Dirk Bowman. Bess was saying something about how she and Dirk could spend the rest of their lives together. "It'll be fantastic, just the two of us, I promise you!" she pleaded, her voice almost cracking. Dirk was completely distracted. He didn't notice anything but the near-hysterical girl in front of him.

Nancy was less than a foot away from him; it was time to make her move. Without warning, she pivoted into a powerful spinning back kick, her heel hitting Dirk's hand. The gun went flying upward, and Nancy moved in slamming her shoulder into Dirk's stomach, pushing him across the room and into a stack of storage crates.

"Somebody get the gun!" Nancy shouted, scrambling off of Dirk.

"Got it!" George called triumphantly, holding the revolver up. "Nice work, Nancy!"

"You taught me that move, remember?" Nancy said. Turning to Bess, she grinned. "I think you missed your calling. You should go on the stage."

Bess laughed. "I just hope I don't have to give any encores. I've never been so scared in my life!"

Kim and Maria were standing over Dirk. "He's out cold," Kim reported. She put an arm around Maria and hugged her. "We're free," she said.

"Yeah, but now what?" George asked.

"What do you mean?" Bess said. "Now we split!"

"No, wait." Nancy thought a minute. "It's not such a great idea for all of us to go trooping up on deck together. I think I'd better scout around first and see what's happening. Maybe I can figure out a way to get us off this boat."

"What about him?" George asked, pointing to Dirk.

"Sit on him if you have to," Nancy replied. "And don't forget, if anybody comes knocking, you've got the gun."

Nancy drew in a deep breath and pushed the door open. She checked the hall, then gave the others a thumbs-up signal and slipped into the empty corridor. She ran silently up the metal stairs.

The *Rosita* had come to a complete stop. Nancy could feel it. She hoped that meant that everybody was gathered on one side of the deck, waiting to be taken to the island. If someone was in the galley, Nancy knew she'd be a sitting duck when she raised that trap door, but there was no way to tell. She'd just have to take her chances.

Cautiously Nancy pushed the door up about half an inch and waited. Nothing. She pushed some more until the opening was big enough for her head. From a distance, she heard the laughter and shouts of people waiting for the launches, but she didn't see anyone in the galley.

It's now or never, she thought, and pushed the door up until the opening was wide enough for her to crawl through. She lowered the door as quietly as possible and then crouched on the floor, waiting.

Nancy didn't know how long the galley would remain empty. She had to get moving or she'd be trapped again. She crept forward, until she could peer around the edge of the entrance.

The partiers were gathered at the railing,

milling around, joking. Nancy didn't see Lila or any of her boys and figured that they were either directing traffic or driving the launches.

Suddenly Nancy realized that a launch was her answer. If she could just get her hands on one of those speedboats, then the five of them might have a chance of breaking free for good.

For a second, Nancy was tempted to join the crowd and lower herself over the side of the *Rosita.* But then she saw one of Lila's boys—the guy who had delivered the flowers—making his way through the party-goers. He moved slowly and casually, smiling at everyone, but his eyes darted swiftly over the faces of the crowd, and Nancy knew that Lila had posted him as a lookout. If Nancy tried to lose herself in the group, he'd spot her. She could just see herself halfway down the rope ladder, trapped in the glare of a powerful flashlight, like an animal paralyzed by the headlights of a car.

But a launch was the only way off the *Rosita,* and Nancy knew she had to get her hands on one. She was trying to figure how when she saw the "florist" making his way toward the galley.

He was fifteen feet away, and Nancy knew there was no going back. In one quick move, she stepped through the galley entrance and slid around to the far side of the deck. Then she waited, heart pounding, listening for a shout, for rapid footsteps that meant he had seen her and was coming after her.

Nothing. Nancy slumped against the outer wall of the galley, knowing she was safe—for the moment. But she couldn't hang around much longer. She had to find a way to get herself and four other people off the boat, or that fancy move she had used to flatten Dirk would turn out to be a total waste.

The noise of the crowd was dying down; it wouldn't be long before everyone was off the boat and on the island. Suddenly, over the sound of the fading laughter, Nancy heard footsteps approaching the galley.

Move! she told herself, and slipped quickly along the rail, glancing over her shoulder every step of the way. She had to find someplace to hide, fast, or she might as well go back down and join the others.

It was as she neared the bow that Nancy saw the metal ladder leading to the top deck. She raced for it, her bare feet almost silent on the deck, and scampered up. She reached the top rung, glanced back, and saw the florist rounding the galley. Nancy gripped the ladder and willed him not to look up.

But apparently Lila's florist was just looking for stray partiers and only glanced carelessly down the passageway before disappearing. Nancy let her breath out and climbed onto the top deck, immediately flattening herself out on her stomach.

The deck was deserted, but Nancy wasn't taking any chances. Still on her stomach, she elbowed her way to the other side and peered over the rail toward the island. Several bonfires had already been started on the beach, and in the glow, Nancy could see a single speedboat heading for the shore. Two others were already tied up just off the beach. The one she was watching must be the last, and she knew it wouldn't be long before the *Rosita* would take off with its human cargo. She had to get her hands on one of those launches, and that meant she had to get to the island— unseen.

Nancy heard a cough, and looking down, saw the florist pacing the deck below. She scrambled back to the far rail and waited to see if he was going to patrol the other side too. As she looked out over the water, it suddenly occurred to her that she could *swim* to the island. It wasn't too far away, and once she got there, she could steal one of the speedboats and zip back to the *Rosita*. She wished she could tell the others to be ready and waiting for her, but she couldn't take the chance of going back down to the hold. She told herself that if the *Rosita* took off before she got back to it, she'd head for Fort Lauderdale and get the police. But she didn't think she'd have to do that. Nancy figured that Lila would need at least half an hour to make sure the island party was going strong before she returned to the *Rosita*.

You can do it, Nancy thought. You have to do it, so don't waste any more time. She got to her knees and looked over the rail, checking to make sure the lower deck was clear. No one was in sight, so Nancy stood up and put her foot on the top rail, gripping it with her toes. She brought her other foot up, found her balance, and slowly straightened to her full height. The water was at least twenty feet below her. Don't think about it, she told herself, just do it.

Nancy raised her arms above her head and pushed out and off the rail, diving headfirst into the dark waters of the Atlantic.

The ocean hit her like a cold slap in the face, and it seemed as if she sank forever before she was able to start pulling herself up. Finally, though, she broke the surface. Gasping, she tossed her hair out of her face and then pulled herself toward the *Rosita*'s stern with strong, steady strokes.

When Nancy reached it, she stopped, treading water. The rail lights and the glow from the bonfires sent a faint path of light along the water, and in that path, about fifteen feet away, Nancy saw a dark triangular shape gliding smoothly through the waves. She wiped her eyes again and blinked, trying to tell herself that she was seeing things.

But she wasn't. The black triangle was a shark's fin, and as Nancy watched, frozen, she saw it swerve sharply and begin to slice through the water, heading straight for her.

Chapter

Fifteen

Nᴀɴᴄʏ ꜰᴇʟᴛ ᴘᴀɴɪᴄ wash over her, colder than the water lapping at her throat. She'd done her share of detective work, but she'd never had to deal with a shark before, and she didn't want to start then.

The shark was swimming closer. Nancy clamped her lips together, forcing back the scream that was threatening to break loose. It would surely attract attention, either the shark's or Lila's, and Nancy wasn't sure which would be worse.

For several minutes, Nancy treaded water, deciding to wait until the shark did whatever it

123

was going to do. But she had no idea what it was going to do, and it probably didn't either, so what was the point? Besides, waiting was just too scary. She had to move or that scream was going to escape her lips.

Not wanting to make any waves, Nancy used just her arms to pull herself smoothly toward the shore. After a moment, she realized she didn't know where the shark was anymore—in front of her, behind her, or below her. Somehow, not knowing was more frightening than knowing, and for a while she kept looking around, trying to locate the telltale fin. But after a few minutes, she simply concentrated on getting ashore. The shark's got the whole ocean to fish in, she kept telling herself. Why should it pick on you?

Avoiding the paths of light cast by the bonfires, Nancy swam in a wide arc, heading for a deserted part of the beach. She thought that once she got there, she could find a subtle way to join the crowd, pretending she'd always been part of it. *If* you get there, she reminded herself, and looked over her shoulder again. She didn't see the shark, but that didn't mean it wasn't lurking somewhere, biding its time.

But Nancy couldn't afford to bide her time. She realized she couldn't keep up the slow pace. She was taking forever to reach the island, and she didn't want to risk letting the *Rosita* get away. Sure, she could send the police after it eventually, but by then it might be too late for the four friends she'd left behind.

Forcing herself to forget every shark movie ever made, Nancy put her head down, started a strong, steady kick with her legs, and shot through the water like an Olympic swimmer going for the gold. She didn't stop until she felt sand grazing her thighs, and even then she didn't stand up. Instead, she crawled out of the water, her stomach brushing the sand, and then flopped down, hoping no one had seen her emerging from the ocean.

When she raised her head and looked toward the party, Nancy realized her fear of being seen was ridiculous. Absolutely nobody was looking her way. They were all too involved in dancing, eating, flirting, and splashing in the water. It would be simple to join them, and since the speedboats were beached close to the party, Nancy knew that was what she had to do.

Confident that no one was watching, Nancy stood up, brushed the sand from her body and picked the seaweed out of her hair. Then she began a slow saunter toward the bonfires, trying to look like she'd been for a solitary stroll along the beach and had decided to rejoin the party.

It was simple, just as she'd thought it would be. The party to nowhere was nothing more than a fancier version of the parties on the Fort Lauderdale beach. The food was a lot better than hot dogs and potato chips, but other than that, it was really just a bunch of people having too good a time to pay any attention to a single girl striding along the sand.

When Nancy reached the thick of the crowd, she put on a smile and started dancing with no one in particular. As she spun to her left, she spotted three of Lila's boys. One was wrapping ears of corn to be roasted in the coals, one was stationed at a table, serving drinks, and the third one—handsome "Mr. Friendly," the maintenance man—was leaning against one of the speedboats, his eyes roving over the crowd. There was no sign of Lila, and Nancy wondered suddenly if she was still on the *Rosita.*

Spinning again so that her back was to the maintenance man, Nancy realized that she had to do something, fast. If Lila was still on the *Rosita,* then the boat might be taking off sooner than Nancy had anticipated. Nancy knew she had to get her hands on one of those launches, but there was no way she could slip past the watchful eye of Mr. Friendly. Somehow, she had to make him leave his post.

Suddenly the group she was with began moving toward the water, and Nancy found herself swept along with them until she was knee-deep in the surf. Splashing each other and laughing as they tried to dance on the shifting sand beneath their feet, they kept moving into deeper water. They were getting farther from the shore and farther, Nancy noticed, from the light cast by the bonfires.

No one was trying to dance anymore; they were all diving under the waves, or swimming lazily. That was when Nancy got her idea. She needed a major distraction, something to get that maintenance man away from the speedboats, and she was going to create it herself.

A wave was rolling in, and Nancy dived under it, surfacing about ten feet from the rest of her group. She checked to make sure no one was paying any attention to her, and then she let out a high-pitched, blood-curdling scream. "Shark!" she shrieked at the top of her lungs, "I see a shark!"

In seconds, everyone had taken up the cry. It didn't seem to matter whether there really was a shark, all that mattered was getting out of the water.

Screaming and shouting, Nancy's group started swimming frantically for the island, while the people on shore raced to the water's edge, yelling for everyone to hurry. When the two groups met on the sand, they all stared out over the dark water, still screaming in fear and excitement.

"I think I see it!" a girl called out. "Look— is that it?"

"It must be!" Nancy answered, not bothering to look. "My gosh, it's huge!"

While everyone stared at the water, Nancy was checking out the launches, and she saw exactly what she'd hoped to see—no maintenance man, no florist, none of Lila's boys. The entire party to nowhere was gathered at the shore, craning their necks for a glimpse of a shark.

This is your chance, Nancy told herself, and it might be the only one you'll get. "There it is!" she shouted, and waited until everyone was looking the other way. Then she turned and raced along the beach toward the speedboats.

When she reached the first one, Nancy ducked behind it and glanced back. The crowd was still at the edge of the water, but no one was screaming anymore, and she knew it would only be a minute or two before they lost interest and started partying again. Two minutes, she thought, that's all you've got.

Her heart pounding, Nancy straightened up and looked into the speedboat. In the glow of the bonfires, she saw something glittering just to the right of the wheel, and let out her breath in a sigh of relief. It was the key. She hadn't even thought about the key, but there it was, thank goodness, ready to ignite the engine.

Keeping low on the sand, Nancy crept to the front of the boat and started pushing. It didn't budge. She shoved harder and when it still didn't move, she realized she'd have to stand up straight if she wanted to shove as hard as she could. She knew she'd be in the full glow of the firelight, and if anyone looked over, they couldn't miss seeing her, but she didn't have a choice. She had to push the boat into the water and get going.

Nancy straightened up and shoved against the boat as hard as she could. It slid two feet forward. Nancy rubbed her palms together and got ready to push again.

Suddenly someone was shouting, and before Nancy had a chance to move, the shout rang out again, loud and clear and furious. It was Lila, standing on the deck of the *Rosita* and pointing straight at Nancy.

"Stop her!" Lila screamed. "She's got a boat! Stop her!"

Nancy spun around to face the crowd of partiers. They were still milling around at the water's edge. All but one. That one—the maintenance man—had broken away from the group and was loping across the sand toward Nancy.

Nancy knew there was no longer any sense in trying to get the boat in the water. She'd never make it. She'd been caught, and as she watched the maintenance man closing the gap between them, she wondered if she'd been caught for good.

For a split second, Nancy stood rooted to the spot and ready to give up. But when she actually heard the sharp, steady breathing of the man, she snapped to attention. Come on, she told herself. You can probably outrun that creep. And if not, you can certainly outthink him!

In a flash, Nancy was off, her heels sending out sprays of sand as she headed away from the boats and the bonfires toward the dark center of the island. She had no idea what she'd find there, but it couldn't be any more dangerous than what she was leaving behind.

Nancy kept running, plunging through the sand until finally the broad, empty stretch of beach gave way to palm trees and under-growth. It was suddenly very dark, which was good, but she couldn't see a thing, and the tangled vines and bushes made it impossible to run quietly, which wasn't so good. She knew she sounded like a scared deer crashing through a forest. She also knew that if Mr. Friendly couldn't see her, he could hear her, since she could certainly hear him, crashing along right behind her, and he was much too close for comfort.

After a few minutes, the clumps of trees started to thin out, and Nancy realized she was heading uphill. She forced herself to keep going, thinking that at least Lila wouldn't take off. She couldn't take that chance, not as long as Nancy was on the run.

Nancy ran until she was no longer under the safe cover of the trees. She burst out into an open space, under a bright moon, and looked around wildly. If she didn't find someplace to hide soon, the maintenance man could just bide his time until she collapsed.

He might already be doing that, Nancy thought. She couldn't hear him anymore, but she knew he couldn't be far behind.

Struggling to keep her balance, Nancy scrambled up a steep incline, and then she stopped, gasping more from fear than from exhaustion. She was on some kind of cliff, and below her—in a sheer, thirty-foot drop—was a smooth stretch of sand, sparkling in the moonlight. Unless she managed to turn herself into a mountain goat, there was no way she could get down.

And at that moment, Nancy heard heavy gasping sounds. The maintenance man. He was closing in fast, and she knew she was too tired to go through another chase scene with him. She would have to face him. Glancing frantically around, she saw three large rocks grouped together. As the breathing grew louder, Nancy rushed over and hid herself behind them.

In seconds, the maintenance man was on

the cliff. As Nancy watched, peering between two of the rocks, he stopped to get his breath, then turned and began walking slowly in Nancy's direction, looking everywhere for signs of the girl he'd been chasing.

Her heart pounding, Nancy made herself wait until he was so close to her hiding place that she could reach out and touch him. Then, in one swift move, her leg shot out, sweeping his feet out from under him, sending him sprawling on the ground.

The maintenance man was caught completely by surprise, and Nancy was just trying to decide what to do with him when she heard a shout. She looked up, and there, on the edge of the cliff in the bright moonlight, stood Dirk Bowman.

Chapter

Sixteen

THE MOMENT NANCY paused, the maintenance man took action, throwing her aside in
one strong movement. Nancy was outnum-
bered, but she wasn't about to give up.

She and the maintenance man faced each
other, squaring off like boxers in the ring. Out
of the corner of her eye, Nancy saw Dirk
Bowman rushing toward them. Lashing out at
the maintenance man with a kick, she spun
around to face Dirk.

But Dirk Bowman ignored Nancy. Instead,
he caught the maintenance man with his left
hand, and, swinging his right arm up from
somewhere around his knees, crashed his fist

squarely into the man's jaw. Lila's boy gasped, sank to his knees, then pitched forward onto his face. He wouldn't be chasing anybody for quite a while.

Stunned, Nancy looked at Dirk, who was rubbing his knuckles and grinning at her. "I've been wanting to do that for a long time," he said.

"Who are you?" Nancy asked warily. "How did you get away? And what happened to my friends?"

"Your friends helped me get away," Dirk told her. "And they're safe. They're waiting for us right now, in the launch we stole. Now come on," he said, reaching for her hand, "let's get going. I'd love to take a nice romantic stroll in the moonlight, but we just don't have time."

Nancy pulled her hand away. "I'm not going anywhere until you tell me who you are."

"I'm a police detective," Dirk said calmly. "I've been working undercover for two months, trying to get enough evidence against Lila to stop her operation for good." He started walking again. "Why don't you walk behind me?" he suggested, grinning at her over his shoulder. "If you think I'm leading you into a trap, you can always jump me again, the way you did on the *Rosita*."

Nancy didn't think she had enough energy left to jump anybody. She really wanted to believe Dirk, but she was still suspicious of him, so she followed his advice and stayed about five feet behind him. "Why didn't you tell me who you were when we first met?" she called out.

"I couldn't risk it," he said. "If my cover had been blown, there would have been no way to stop Lila. Besides, the lady would probably have killed me."

"But you knew what was going on," Nancy reminded him. "Wasn't that enough evidence?"

"We suspected, we didn't know for sure. We needed witnesses," he explained. "And even after I started working for Lila, it was a long time before she trusted me with her little secret. In fact," he said with a laugh, "you and your friends were my first assignment."

"Me and my friends?" Nancy asked. "What about before that? What about my windsurfing accident? You didn't have anything to do with that?"

"Nope. My guess is that one of Lila's boys saw us together and reported it to her, and she told him to take care of you," Dirk said. "She still didn't trust me then. But I put on a pretty convincing act, and finally she decided I was okay."

"So tonight, when you came down to the hold, you were supposed to kill us, right?" Nancy asked.

"Right." Dirk stopped and turned, looking at Nancy. "I wasn't going to follow Lila's orders, of course. But Bess never gave me a chance to tell you that, and when I came to, you'd already taken off for the island. How did you get here, anyway?"

"I swam!" Quickly Nancy told him everything that had happened since she'd escaped from the *Rosita*.

As Dirk listened his eyes lit up in admiration, and when she finished he gave a low whistle. "You're really something, Detective." He held out his hand, and Nancy shook it.

"But just think," he went on, his eyes twinkling mischievously, "if you hadn't knocked me out, you could have saved yourself that swim."

Nancy started to argue, but when she caught the look in his eyes, she found herself laughing instead. He grabbed her other hand, and the two of them began running together.

Soon they were back in the trees, and it wasn't long before Nancy heard the distant strains of rock music and laughter from the party to nowhere. Halfway back to the shore, Dirk started heading to the right. "The launch is around a curve in the beach," he told Nancy. "We'll use the trees for cover."

"How did you get it there without anyone hearing the motor?" Nancy asked.

"Kim navigated and the rest of us paddled,"

Dirk replied with a laugh. "We made a great team. The only thing we really had to worry about was Lila spotting us from the *Rosita*. But I guess she was too busy making sure you were brought back to notice us."

"She must be wondering what's taking that guy so long," Nancy said. "She's probably getting very antsy."

Dirk laughed again. "Wait'll I come after her with four or five other cops. Then she'll know what antsy really is!"

Nancy began to forget about sore feet and sore muscles. She forgot about everything but leaving the island, and when they finally caught sight of the sleek little speedboat waiting a few feet from the shoreline, she grabbed Dirk's hand again and pulled him along behind her as she broke into a run.

"Finally!" Bess's voice cried out. "We've been sitting in this boat so long I was beginning to grow barnacles!"

Nancy laughed and splashed into the water. "You think *you've* had it bad," she joked as she reached the boat. "Wait'll you hear what *I've* been through!"

There was no time to exchange stories, though. In spite of what Dirk had said, he and Nancy knew that Lila wouldn't wait forever. If she discovered that they'd escaped, she might just take off, maybe for another country. That would leave the police with no one to arrest but her troop of handsome boys. Dirk didn't want that, and neither did Nancy. They both wanted Lila Templeton caught.

Quickly Nancy, Dirk, and George pushed the speedboat far enough out so they could lower the engine into the water. When they climbed in, Dirk slid into the driver's seat and turned the key. The engine caught with a roar, and as the boat pulled smoothly away from the island, the six passengers laughed with relief.

"I never thought I'd say it," Bess admitted, "but I'll actually be glad to get back to River Heights."

"But you haven't fallen in love yet," George teased. "Are you sure you don't want to stick around?"

"No thanks!" Bess said. "There are plenty of guys at home."

"Hey, what about me?" Dirk joked. "I thought you said you'd spend the rest of your life with me if I just got you off the *Rosita*."

Bess giggled, and leaning forward, planted a kiss on his cheek. "You're fantastic, Dirk," she told him, "but I'm afraid that was a promise I just can't keep."

Everyone laughed again, but Nancy stopped suddenly as she became aware of another sound. Even over the whine of the speedboat, she could hear it—a heavy throbbing, almost a rumbling, like a powerful motor. She glanced around. Maria was staring out the back of the boat, her eyes wide with fear.

"Maria?" Nancy said. "What is it? What do you see?"

"Look," Maria said, pointing. "She's found us!"

Straining to see, Nancy could just make out a large, dark shape looming behind them. It didn't stay dark for long, though. As Nancy watched, the deck and rail lights of the *Rosita* flashed on.

The *Rosita* was only about a hundred feet away, its powerful engines louder than ever as Lila Templeton aimed it straight at the tiny speedboat.

Bess stood halfway up and let out a scream. "She's going to ram us!"

"I'm afraid that's exactly what she has in mind," Dirk agreed. "And if she gets close enough, she'll probably take a few shots at us, too. The lady is definitely desperate."

"I thought the party was over," George said grimly, "but it looks like it's just getting started."

The speedboat was fast, but so was the *Rosita,* and as the six of them watched, Lila's powerful boat surged through the water, shortening the gap between them.

"Can't we go any faster?" Nancy called to Dirk.

"Not much," he told her. Slipping an arm around her shoulder, he pulled her head close to his lips, speaking quietly so the others wouldn't hear. "We're low on gas," he said, "and I'm not sure how long we'll last if she decides to chase us all over the Atlantic."

Shivering with tension, Nancy stared at the gas gauge. The arrow was hovering around the one-quarter mark. It might be enough to get them back to Fort Lauderdale, but only if they made a beeline for it. If they had to do many fancy maneuvers to get away from Lila, they'd never make it.

At that moment, Nancy heard a faint popping sound, something like a firecracker. She turned and saw one of Lila's boys on the top deck of the *Rosita*. He was braced against the rail like a sharpshooter, aiming a long-barreled rifle at the six people in the speedboat.

"Everybody, down!" Nancy shouted.

"If they get much closer, he'll be able to pick us off one by one!" Bess cried out, as she huddled in the bottom of the boat.

"Us or the engine!" George exclaimed. "And if he hits the engine, there won't be anything left of us to pick off!"

Dirk fumbled around on the floor and pulled up the revolver that Nancy had kicked out of his hand a few hours before. "It's hardly a rifle," he commented wryly, "but it's better than nothing!"

Nancy nodded and reached for his hand, pulling him up. "You deal with Lila," she suggested, "and leave the driving to me."

Dirk nodded and crawled to the back of the boat, while Nancy slid into the driver's seat. The fuel gauge was just under the quarter mark by then, and she knew she didn't have much time. Glancing back, she saw that the *Rosita* hadn't gained on them, but she also saw that Lila wasn't directly behind them anymore. She'd pulled the *Rosita* out, so that it was between the speedboat and the mainland.

Wiping the spray from her face, Nancy pushed the stick up a notch, giving the boat more power. It slapped over the water like a roller-coaster car, but Nancy could still hear the throbbing of the *Rosita*'s engines, and she knew that Lila was keeping up with her.

"I could go around behind them!" she shouted to Dirk. "The *Rosita* can't turn as fast as we can!"

"Try it!" he called back. "Just be careful of sandbars. They're all over the place!"

Now he tells me, Nancy thought. She checked the fuel again and decided to risk the extra mileage. Getting a good grip on the wheel, she cut it sharply, turning the boat so that it was heading back toward the *Rosita*. As they passed the *Rosita*'s bow, Nancy saw Lila's boy leave his post and scramble toward the stern, rifle in hand.

Suddenly the *Rosita* began to turn toward the mainland. She knows what I'm trying to do, Nancy thought. She's going to cut me off if she can!

Nancy turned the wheel again and felt the boat begin to bounce wildly as it cut across the *Rosita*'s wake. Both boats were heading for the mainland, but Lila's had a slight lead, and she'd angled it toward the speedboat. If she managed to get much farther ahead, she *would* be able to cut them off, and Nancy knew they didn't have enough gas left to try any more tricks.

The spray was practically blinding her, and her hands were so wet they kept slipping off the wheel, but Nancy wiped her face and eyes and tried frantically to see exactly what was ahead of her. All she had to light her way were the moon and the dim glow from the *Rosita*.

Suddenly though, they were all Nancy needed. Ahead of her, stretching across the water like a pale ribbon, was one of the sandbars Dirk had warned her about. It seemed to go on forever, and Nancy knew that if she tried to zip around it, she'd crash into the *Rosita* going one way, or run out of gas going the other.

Bess had crawled up beside her, and Nancy could tell from the look on her face that she'd seen the sandbar too. Her teeth chattering with fear, Bess tried to smile. "Wouldn't it be nice if this boat had wings?" she asked.

"That's it!" Nancy cried out.

"What's it?"

"Wings!" Nancy grinned and pushed Bess back down. "Hang on, everybody," she shouted, "we're going to fly!"

Nancy gripped the wheel and eased the stick up to full speed. As the little boat shot forward with all the power its engine could give it, Nancy gritted her teeth and aimed it straight for the sandbar.

Chapter
Seventeen

THE FRONT OF the speedboat hit the sand with a bone-jarring thump. Then, its blade stirring the air, it sailed up and over the sandbar, splashed down hard on the other side, and sped on toward the lights of Fort Lauderdale.

As soon as they caught their breath, everyone turned to look behind them, and what they saw made them cheer out loud. Lila was trying to avoid the sandbar, but she was moving too fast, and as the six people in the speedboat looked on, the *Rosita* plowed straight into it. Its engines grinding uselessly,

Lila's boat came to a dead stop. Lila was trapped, and her party was finally over.

"Nancy, you did it!" George shouted.

"That was one nice piece of driving, Detective," Dirk said with a grin.

Nancy laughed. "Thanks. Just don't ask me to do it again!"

"Being stuck out there serves Lila right," Bess said. "I just hope there's no way she can escape."

"Uh-oh, I just thought of something," Nancy said. "I'll bet the *Rosita* has lifeboats. That means Lila *does* have a way to escape. And you can bet she'll use it."

"She couldn't get very far, but you're right, Nancy," Dirk agreed, "she's not the kind to give up until every last door's been slammed in her face."

"I don't think even that would make her give up," George commented. "Not when she's as desperate as she is right now."

There was no time to waste. As soon as they were safely back to shore, Dirk raced for the nearest phone and called in his backup team to help capture Lila and her crew. Nancy and the others hopped into their rental car and rushed Kim back to the hospital.

"I wanted to stick around and see them bring Lila in," Kim protested on the way. "Honestly, I'm perfectly fine!"

145

"You might be fine," Nancy told her, "but your mother's probably having a nervous breakdown by now."

"That's right," Bess said. "She wasn't even with us when we left the hospital before, so she's still completely in the dark. She must be frantic!"

Bess was right. When they got to the hospital, they found Mrs. Baylor still frantic with worry, and the entire staff in an uproar over the missing patient. As soon as Kim appeared, the doctors whisked her away to check on her condition, and finally her mother calmed down enough to listen to what had happened.

When Nancy finished telling the story, Mrs. Baylor sighed in relief. "Thank goodness you were here, Nancy, and that it's over!"

"That's exactly what I was thinking," Bess said with a yawn.

"Well, it's not quite over," Nancy reminded them. "We'll all have to give statements to the police. And if there's a trial, Kim and Maria will probably have to testify."

"I will be very happy to do that," Maria said. "Even if it means that I can't stay here. I want to see Lila Templeton get . . ." she searched for the right words.

"Get what's coming to her!" Bess finished with a laugh.

"You're very brave, Maria," Nancy said. "I

hope things work out for you so you don't have to go back to your country if you don't want to."

One of the doctors came in then and gave them the good news—Kim was weak and worn out, but otherwise she seemed to be fine. They just wanted to keep her in the hospital for a couple of days to make sure.

Leaving Maria at the hospital with Kim's mother, Nancy, Bess, and George sped back to the docks just in time to see the police patrol boat arrive. A very happy looking Dirk Bowman waved to them from the deck, then pointed to a small group of people—it was Lila Templeton and her handsome, deadly crew, looking very *un*happy.

The sun was just coming up as Nancy, Bess, and George let themselves into their room at the Surfside Inn. They took turns in the shower, and then George and Nancy started packing. But Bess wrapped a towel around her wet head and flopped down on the cot.

"I've never been so exhausted in my entire life," she yawned. "Nobody wake me for at least twelve hours."

"Sorry," George told her, "but our plane leaves in four hours. You don't want to miss it, do you?"

"I don't know," Bess said. "Now that everything's over, I wouldn't mind sticking around for a couple of days. There *are* a lot of cute guys around and I'd hate to miss out."

Nancy laughed. "I thought you said there were plenty of guys back home," she teased.

"That was when I thought I was going to die," Bess protested. "But now that Lila and her crew are behind bars, I figure I might as well enjoy the rest of spring break."

"I would have given anything to see the look on Lila's face when the police came to 'rescue' her," George said. "I wonder if she tried to lie her way out of it."

"If she did, it didn't do her any good," Nancy said. "Not with Kim and Maria and Dirk as witnesses against her."

"Speaking of Dirk," George said, peering out the window, "he just pulled up in that fancy red car of his, and it looks like he's heading this way."

Nancy opened the door and smiled as she watched Dirk Bowman come down the hall. "I thought you'd at least take the rest of the day off," she said.

"The day? I'm taking a week off," he replied with a grin. "But I knew you were leaving, and I had a couple of things I wanted to tell you. How about a quick walk?"

Nancy slipped on a pair of sandals, and together she and Dirk strolled down the sidewalk in the early morning sun.

"First," Dirk said, reaching for Nancy's hand, "I've got some good news. Kim's mother agreed to vouch for Maria and get her a job with some friends here in Fort Lauderdale. So she'll be staying on, and she says she's going to start college as soon as she can. She wants to be an engineer."

"That's great," Nancy said with relief. "I was worried that she'd be sent back." She stifled a yawn and then laughed. "Sorry. I'm completely wiped out."

"Well, that's the second thing I wanted to talk to you about," Dirk said. He stopped walking and put his hands on her shoulders. "I wanted to thank you, Detective. You were fantastic. And if you ever come back to Fort Lauderdale, let me know." Bending down, he touched his lips softly to Nancy's. "Thanks to you, Lila Templeton won't be throwing any more parties."

For a moment, Nancy leaned her head against his shoulder, smiling. Then, with a gasp, she suddenly pulled away.

"What's wrong?" Dirk asked.

"I just remembered," Nancy said, trying not to laugh. "The party. The party to nowhere! All those people are still stranded out there on that island!"

Dirk's blue eyes widened in shock, and he shook his head. "I guess I'll start my vacation this afternoon," he said. He gave Nancy a quick kiss and then raced off to his car. "See what I mean?" he called back over his shoulder. "I could use you down here, Detective!"

Laughing, Nancy watched the red car speed down the palm-lined street. Then she headed back to her hotel. It was time to go home.

Nancy's next case:

After a vacation like this, Nancy *needs* a rest! A white water rafting trip with Ned, George, and Bess, looks like the perfect way to get away from it all.

But someone has other plans—deadly plans.

First, the rafting party is stranded in the wilderness. Is this any way to run a vacation? One girl thinks so—all she wants to do is flirt with Ned.

But there's a maniac loose in the woods, whose mind is *not* on romance but on murder. And the main target seems to be Nancy Drew! In *WHITE WATER TERROR*, Case #6 in *The Nancy Drew Files*™.

THE HARDY BOYS® CASE FILES

Simon & Schuster Mall Order
200 Old Tappan Rd., Old Tappan, N.J. 07675

Please send me the books I have checked above. I am enclosing $_____ (please add $0.75 to cover the postage and handling for each order. Please add appropriate sales tax). Send check or money order—no cash or C.O.D.'s please. Allow up to six weeks for delivery. For purchase over $10.00 you may use VISA: card number, expiration date and customer signature must be included.

Name _____

Address _____

City _____ State/Zip _____

VISA Card # _____ Exp.Date _____

Signature _____

762-13